Sweet Danger

EROTIC STORIES OF FORBIDDEN DESIRE FOR COUPLES

Sweet Danger

EROTIC STORIES OF FORBIDDEN DESIRE FOR COUPLES

EDITED BY

VIOLET BLUE

CLEIS
PRESS

Published in the United States by Cleis Press, Inc., 2246 Sixth Street, Berkeley, California 94710.

Printed in the United States.
Cover design: Scott Idleman/Blink
Cover photograph: April/Getty Images
Text design: Frank Wiedemann
Cleis Press logo art: Juana Alicia
10 9 8 7 6 5 4 3 2 1

ISBN: 978-1-57344-648-8

Contents

Introduction
For You. I Would.

Love games. Erotic risk—and reward. The anxieties of lust impinging the walled garden of domesticity.

Sweet Danger collects the stories of love's sex games taken to their limits—but not outside the limits of reason. The ways these very-much-in-love couples play together are not the light and soft games you'd find in a collection that was afraid of the dark: these lovers are so crazy about each other, they take their most intense fantasies into real life and do it with the lights on. And sometimes they do it in public.

Best of all, these stories are realistic, loving, and extremely hard-core all at the same time. I wanted to see the most pornographic taboos a couple could try out together done with the most romantic trappings and the utmost realism. The highly-skilled authors I handpicked for this book delivered.

I wanted our dangerous dance with sexual taboo writ big, in detail, for people as discriminating as myself. Some of the stories will shock you; the love here courts just as much danger as do the sexual scenarios depicted. We're moths to the flame of sexual taboo. I wanted to go there, and give you something you could use, in as many ways as you want.

Many books attempt to understand our attraction to sexual taboo, but here is one that feeds you ideas for sexual taboos like fingers full of frosting. *Sweet Danger* gives you a front seat to watch those taboos being played out in all their sexual delirium, erotic danger, and sweetly explicit detail. This book can show you how to make your most taboo erotic fantasies come true; its twenty superbly written short stories feature couples who want it so bad they can taste it. And they do, over and over again.

Sexual taboo will never go out of style. While books, talk shows, women's and men's magazines, and even pop stars court a veritable A–Z sideshow of sexual taboos that come and go like seasons, our attraction to the sweeter dangers found at the edges of love and lust will always stop us in our tracks.

When you're in love, why would you take a risk? Perhaps it's the safety of love, or equally, the heady rush of lust that makes us bold enough to say, "I want to. With you." In love we become each other's most prized—and privileged—possession. This is what makes it okay to try scenes that screen like a filmstrip in our heads, that we replay in our most delightfully filthy fantasy moments for our own private peep-show pleasures: the safety of private fantasy, the solitude of sinking into sexual taboo. But the power of two changes all that, ripping open the doors to hold hands and jumping in the fantasy together—even if just by reading these stories aloud to each other.

But there's something else about our edgy sexual fantasies, the magnetic pull to taboo that engages more than brain and body parts below the belt. Taboo shared by two is a risk of the heart. And when presented with possibility, trust, and lust, it is a sumptuous buffet for the starving, something we simply cannot resist. Like the couples skipping and holding hands and laughing and playing and having soul-touching orgasms at the edge of sexual safety, it's a sweet danger that completes us, brings us closer to true love.

The question between lovers becomes: how far, and how much would you risk to prove your love? What would you tell me that you can tell no one else, the gift of sexual secrecy that is just for me, the thing you can trust me with the most, that I can be the one with the key to really turn you on and get you off? And your desire: how far will you go to show me that I'm the one you lust the most, so much you would do anything to have me up against the car in a public parking lot, to rip my clothes, just to taste me? How far will your lust go—for *me*?

And if we got caught—would you save me?

When we share sexual taboo, whether it's sexual danger of the heart or of the body, or just in fantasy and emotion, we have the chance to become—and find—the hero of our hearts.

That's what pulled me to assemble this collection of stories: smokin', sweet, edgy taboos filled with hot fantasies for those looking to find new ideas, practical details if you want to try them "at home," and that smart combo of superb writing and explicit sex you've come to expect from the high-quality erotic anthologies that win awards for my talented authors and me. I've worked closely with each of these writers, from bestseller to novice, to make every detail realistic, each taboo stunningly wicked yet entirely possible to recreate in real life, and to ensure the sex you'll read is among the hottest you'll find in print.

Welcome to *Sweet Danger*. The couples whose deep-est, darkest, sweetest, and naughtiest fantasies are played out within these pages are committed to one another without question. They take sex, lust, and fantasy as far as it will go, just to please each other and get off together—and they take their sexual taboos to the very limit. And for some it's only the beginning. Take Donna George Storey's "Picture Perfect," where a shy couple begins making home videos for a wealthy sophisticate, awakening something they never knew existed between them. Next, in "Old Friends" by N.T. Morley, when an old friend comes to visit his girlfriend, the male protagonist hopes to see his sexy wife in a threesome with the beautiful stranger—but what they have in mind goes far beyond what anyone might guess. Name a forbidden fantasy, and you'll sink into an expert scenario, such as M. Christian's "Alice," where a man's man finds a delicious release and a couple opens a dar-ing new vista when he becomes the girl she's always wanted to seduce. And there is so much more.

Every fantasy here is familiar, but each has so many layers and smart twists it's impossible to say you can predict anything the characters will do, or what's gone on behind the scenes (until the sweet revelings, of course—as in life, every fantasy starts with a confession). Several of the taboos found here take a common fantasy, or typical taboo, and turn it on its head. Fancy a cuckold, but find the thought of cheating distasteful in real life? Stories like Jolie Joss's "Pearl Necklace" were written just for you. If your furtive imagination flashes intense group sex moments, then marvel at how lovingly con-structed a rough-trade gang bang is detailed in Eric Emerson's "Greedy."

FOR YOU. I WOULD.

Some of these sexual fantasies are not for the faint of heart, yet are carefully laid traps that mingle our forbidden fantasies with pure, unfettered lust. In "Dress Me Up" by Erica Dumas, a woman is kept on the erotic edge throughout dinner, then compelled into a situation rife with public sexual humiliation and rough sex with strangers. "Medical Attention" by Skye Black takes a woman's medical fantasies as far as they can go—then further. And in Thomas S. Roche's "Cocked and Loaded," what begins with a day at the shooting range climaxes at home when dominance and submission become the target for a couple who get off with intense edge play.

Each of these stories is remarkable: hot and very explicit sex, loving couples, realistic details, distinctive and unforgettable writing, and over twenty taboos—where no one is hurt, exploited, or in danger, and everyone gets off. The book is remarkable, too, especially when you consider the high caliber talents of famous erotica writers like M. Christian, Thomas S. Roche, Sarah Sands, Donna George Storey, P. S. Haven, Felix D'Angelo, Elizabeth Colvin, Saskia Walker, and many others. It's a collection I'm proud to have curated, and enjoyed. I hope you enjoy these little tastes of *Sweet Danger* as much as I do.

Violet Blue
San Francisco

Picture Perfect

DONNA GEORGE STOREY

I didn't mean to shave it all off. At first I was trying for a whimsical heart shape, but I couldn't seem to get the curves even. Then I sculpted a fur patch like those models in men's magazines, but it looked too much like Hitler's mustache. In the end I went all the way—the Greek statue look. It's harder than you think to get yourself all smooth down there. I stood with one leg propped up on the side of the tub, studying my cunt like exam notes. I'd never looked at myself so carefully down there before. What surprised me was the color—the deep, almost shocking pink of the inner lips. The skin looked so sensitive and dewy, I was scared to get close with that nasty razor, so I left a little fringe. There was no room for mistakes.

I called Brian at work to tell him about my art project.

"Hey, Kira." I knew someone was in his office by his offhand tone, but I went ahead and told him anyway.

"I just shaved my pussy."

There was a pause.

"Oh, is that so? Listen, honey, I'm in the middle of a meeting right now. I'll call you back when I can. Okay?" Only a wife would have picked up the faint tremor in his voice.

Unfortunately, Brian was a model employee—not the type who would stand up in front of the boss and announce, "Sorry, I have to go. My wife just shaved her pussy." It would probably be hours before he could get home. That left a whole afternoon alone, just me and my bald snatch.

I went over to the full-length mirror. My heart was pounding. I hadn't felt this naughty since I was a teenager doing "homework" up in my bedroom with my panties around one ankle and a pillow pushed between my legs, ear cocked for the sound of my mother's footsteps in the hall. Which was silly because I was alone in my own house and all I was doing was looking at myself, my new self: the white triangle of smooth skin, the fold of tender pink flesh now visible between the lips. There was an indentation at the top of the slit, as if someone had pressed a finger into it. I had an overwhelming urge to play with myself. Just an appetizer before I jumped Brian's bones tonight. I touched a tentative finger to my clit. I was already wet.

The phone rang.

"I'm taking the afternoon off," Brian told me. His voice was husky. "I'll be home in twenty minutes. Don't you dare touch that shaved pussy of yours until I get there."

When I hung up, I had to laugh. My husband knew me well. Very well.

There were no *hi-honey* kisses or *how-was-your-day*; the moment Brian got through the door, he pushed me back on the sofa and yanked open my robe. He made a little sound in his throat, half gasp, half moan.

"Wow, you really did a job on it."

I smiled. "Didn't you believe me?"

He gaped, eyes glowing. *Pussy power*—suddenly the words took on fresh meaning. Gently he nudged my thighs apart. I shivered. He bent down. I thought—and hoped—he was going to kiss me there.

"You didn't get all the hair off."

"Hey, it's a tricky job."

He frowned. "Don't move."

He left me lying on the sofa with my legs spread like a virgin sacrifice. My pussy was getting chilly, but my breath was coming fast and I had that naughty teenage feeling again, arousal so sharp it was almost pain.

Brian returned with a towel, a canister of shaving cream, and a razor. He'd changed into his bathrobe, which did nothing to hide his bobbing erection. He came back again with a basin of water, which he set carefully on the coffee table. The last trip brought the video camera and tripod.

I felt a contraction low in my belly.

"Spread your legs wider."

I caught my breath, but obeyed.

He patted a dab of shaving cream between my legs. The coolness made me squirm.

"Lie still."

He was acting awfully bossy, but I didn't want any slipups. I held my thighs to keep them from shaking.

"Relax, Kira," Brian said, more kindly. Guys are always saying that when they're about to mess around with your private parts. Still Brian did have plenty of experience with shaving, so I closed my eyes and took a deep breath. The room was quiet, except for the scraping sound of the razor and the occasional swish of water. At last he rinsed me with a washcloth, smiling as I wriggled under his vigorous assault.

He leaned close to examine his work.

"Picture perfect," he declared.

Five minutes later, I was sitting naked in our armchair, watching my own twat, larger than life on our new plasma TV screen. My legs were modestly pressed together, but Brian had me lounge back so you could see the slit, shorn of its covering. He knelt, pointing the camera straight at me.

"Did you get turned on when you were shaving?" His tone was soothing now, like a friendly interviewer on a weekly news magazine.

"Yes," I admitted in a small voice.

"Did you masturbate?"

"No." A few flicks didn't count, right?

"You wanted to, though."

I swallowed.

Brian clicked his tongue. "Why don't you do it now? Don't you want to know if it feels different when it's shaved?"

My cheeks burned, but I ignored the question and turned to the screen. "It sure looks different."

"Yeah. It really does look like lips. The skin gets pinker here and pouts." He reached over and pinched the edges.

I bit back a moan.

"We could put lipstick on it. Deep red like a forties movie star."

"No, that's too weird," I said and immediately regretted it. Why was I being such a prude? After all, I'd started this with my little experiment in the tub. Suddenly bold, I glided my middle finger up and down along the groove. "This is an easier way to make it redder."

Brian grinned. "Yes, indeed. Let's get the full view." The camera zoomed in expectantly.

I hesitated. I'd played with myself in front of Brian before, but now a stranger was in the room with us, a stranger with a round, staring eye. "Go ahead, honey. I know you're turned on. Your chest is all flushed." I inched my thighs open, glancing at the TV. To my embarrassment I was already quite ruddy down there and shiny-slick with pussy juice. The fleshy folds and hole filled up the screen. My finger, laboring at my clit, looked strangely small.

"Does it feel different?" Brian was back to being the cordial journalist.

"A little."

"Tell me."

"The mound is really smooth, like satin."

"Is it more sensitive?"

"Yes, I think so. The outer lips are tingling. Or maybe I'm just noticing it more." I looked up at him. "What's with all the questions? You sound like you're interviewing my pussy for a dirty documentary."

Brian laughed. "What if I was?"

"Now wait a minute." I sat up and snapped my legs together.

5

He turned the camera to my face. A frowning twin gazed back at me from the TV.

Brian, on the other hand, was still smiling. "What if there was a guy in the city, a dot-com billionaire, who collects videos of married ladies pleasuring themselves?"

My pulse jumped. "You're joking right?"

"For his eyes only, discretion guaranteed. He pays well for it."

"Oh, yeah? How much?"

"Three grand for a genuine orgasm. That won't be a problem for you. We might get even more because you're all shaved down there. Just think, Kira, we could go on a nice vacation for a few very pleasant minutes of work." I moaned and covered my face with my hands.

"Don't worry. I'll edit this part out. He specifically requested no faces. Just sweet pussy."

Would my own husband really sell some rich voyeur a movie of me masturbating? I never thought he had it in him. And I never thought I'd find the idea so fiercely arousing. Funny all the things you discover when you shave your pussy.

Brian put the camera on standby. His eyes twinkled. "Jake and Ashley did it."

"No way."

"Lie back. I'll tell you about it."

There I was with my pussy on the screen again, a sprawled-leg Aphrodite, her naughty parts tinted dark rose.

"Ashley let Jake talk her into this?"

"Better than that. She went with him to drop it off. The guy tacks on a bonus if the lady and her husband join him for a drink."

I pictured Brian's best friend's wife, with her spiky blonde hair and lip ring, swishing up the stairs of a mansion in a black party dress and heels. That wasn't so hard to believe. "What was the rich guy like? I bet he was a creep."

"Jake said he was the perfect gentleman. Fortyish. Friendly. He served them a glass of champagne and hors d'oeuvres made by his personal chef. They chatted a bit, then left with an envelope of cash. Easiest money they ever made."

"I don't think I could meet him." So why did I see myself walking up those same mansion steps, Brian at my side, video in hand? I wasn't as wild as Ashley. I'd have on something prim: a lace blouse, a velvet choker with a cameo, a long skirt. I'd wear my hair up and keep my eyes down, blushing under his billion-dollar gaze. The perfect lady. That rich guy would get a boner the size of Florida just looking at me.

"Jake said the guy only did one thing that crossed the line. When they were leaving he took Ashley's right hand and kissed it like he was a baron or something."

"What's wrong with kissing her hand?" I had a weakness for old-fashioned manners.

"Well, it's the hand she uses to masturbate, of course. Like you're doing right now."

Without my realizing it, my hand had wandered back down between my legs. I jerked it away.

Brian laughed. Holding the camera steady, he reached up and guided my fingers back to my pussy. "Don't be bashful, honey. He wants to watch you do it. So do I."

And the truth was, I wanted them to see, the two pairs of eyes floating before me, Brian's the greenish-gray of a northern sea, the rich guy's golden and glittering.

"Where does he watch it? In his home theater?" Under the veil of my lashes I studied the screen. My labia jiggled lewdly as my finger strummed on. That's what the rich guy would see as he sat on his leather couch in his silk dressing gown. A wine-colored gown, the same color as his swollen dick. He'd pull it out and stroke it as he watched.

"A home theater, yes," Brian said softly. "State of the art."

"Why are you doing this? Don't you care if your wife shows her cunt to some horny billionaire?" The words came in gasps.

"The joke's on him. We'll take his money and get a suite in the fanciest hotel in town and fuck all night." Brian sounded winded, too, as if he'd just finished a run. Then I realized he was jerking off.

"I'm not a whore." I was half-sobbing, from shame and pleasure.

"Of course you're not, honey. You're a nice, pretty married lady. That's what he wants. Someone he'd glimpse at the gourmet grocery store or the espresso bar, buying a nonfat decaf cappuccino. I see guys staring at you. If only they knew the truth about my sweet-faced angel. If only they knew you want it so bad you shave your pussy and let men take pictures of it."

Sounds were coming out of my throat, sounds I'd never made before, high-pitched whines and animal moans.

"You're the hottest thing he's ever seen, but no matter how much he pays he can never have the real you."

"Oh, god, I'm gonna come," I whimpered.

A hand closed around my wrist and wrenched it away.

"He'll pay an extra thousand if you come while we fuck."

"Did Ashley do it?" I panted. I knew what the answer would be.

"Jake said she had the best orgasm of her life."

Brian hurriedly fixed the camera to the tripod, adjusted the height, then lifted me to my feet and took my place on the chair.

"Face the camera," he said.

My knees were as soft as melted caramel, but by gripping the arms of the chair I managed to position myself properly. On the screen Brian's penis reared up, my smooth snatch hovering above.

"Sit on it."

I lowered myself onto him with a sigh. Then I was up again, a woman who couldn't make up her mind. Up or down? It was there in full color: Brian's rod plunging in and out, his balls dangling beneath like a small pink pillow. "Now turn around and ride me."

In a daze I straddled him, my knees digging into the cushion. Just last week, we'd done it this way on the sofa. We pretended it was prom night, and we were sneaking a midnight quickie while my parents snored in the bedroom upstairs.

"Do you like to fuck with a shaved twat?"

"Yes," I confessed. "I like to rub my bare lips on you." Which was exactly what I was doing, lingering on the downstroke to grind my exposed clit against the rough hairs at the base of his cock.

"You're so wet. That rich guy can hear it. Your hungry lips gobbling up my cock."

Brian began to twist my nipples between his fingers.

"It's an extra five hundred if you show him your asshole."

I grunted assent and bucked harder. In that position, the rich guy could see it anyway.

Then he whispered in my ear, "And another five hundred if you let me touch it."

I froze mid-thrust. "Please, Brian, don't," I whispered back. I didn't want the rich guy to hear. We'd recently discovered that when Brian diddles my butt crack when we fuck, it feels like a second clit. I loved it, but I was embarrassed and wanted it to be our secret. Brian knew he could make me blush just talking about it.

"Why not, baby? Because he'll know you're a bad girl who comes when I play with your pretty ass?"

"Please," I begged. My asshole, however, seemed to have other ideas, the brazen little show-off, pushing itself out, all plumped and ticklish.

"Please what, Kira? I know you want it, but I won't touch it until you say yes."

"Please," I gasped. "Yes."

"That's a good girl. Nice and polite."

Good girl, bad girl, I wasn't sure what I was, but it didn't matter. My torso rippled like a column of heat between his hands, one tweaking my nipple, the other going to town on my quivering bottom. Our bodies made rude noises, swampy, squishy sounds—or was it the rich guy whacking off? He probably used a special custom-made lotion to make his dick all slippery. He'd be close to the end now, pumping his fist faster and faster, his single nether eye weeping a tear of delight. He'd gotten everything he wanted. The cool lady in the gourmet grocery store was unzipped and undone, a bitch in heat, writhing shamelessly on her husband's cock for his viewing pleasure.

But I had one little surprise left for him.

"What if you spank it? Is that another thousand?"

"Two thousand." I could tell Brian was close, too.

"I want him to see it. Spank my naughty asshole," I yelled, so the rich guy could hear.

The first slap sent a jolt straight through me that quickly dissolved into pleasure, foamy fingers of a wave creeping into the hollows of my body.

"Again."

Smack.

Each blow hammered me deeper onto Brian's cock. I pushed my ass out to take the next one, to show that rich guy I could do it. He was so turned on, I could feel his eyes burning into my back through the screen. But it wasn't just him. There were others watching—my parents, my tenth-grade science teacher, the postal clerk who sneaks glances at my tits, a Supreme Court Justice or two—dozens of them, their faces twisted into masks of shock and fascination. And beneath, in the shadows, hands were stroking hard-ons or shoved into panties, damp and fragrant with arousal. They liked it, all of them, and I was watching them as they watched me in an endless circle of revelation and desire.

"I'm...gonna...come."

"Come for him. Now!" Brian bellowed. The last slaps fell like firecrackers snapping, and I jerked my hips to their rhythm as my climax tore through my belly. With the chair springs squeaking like crazy and Brian grunting, *fuck your shaved pussy, fuck it,* that rich guy got himself quite a show.

I'd say it was worth every penny.

Afterward, I pulled Brian down to the carpet with me. Our profiles filled the screen. He'd seen me and I'd seen him and we fit so well together and I loved him more than anything. I told him that. Or maybe I just kissed him, a deep soul kiss that lasted a long, long time.

The rich guy got that part for free.

Old Friends
N. T. MORLEY

"Are you excited to finally meet Gina?" asked Brooke.

"Yeah," I said, not sounding very convincing.

"I'm sure you two will hit it off," said my wife, beaming broadly. There was the faintest hint of mischief in her look, and I wondered what was going on in her head. Then Gina walked off the plane, and my eyes went wide.

Of course, I'd seen pictures of my wife's best friend from college. Early in our relationship, Brooke had subjected me to every last snapshot, leading me through her big books of photos in that way new girlfriends sometimes do. I'd seen pictures of Brooke and Gina frolicking on the beach, bikini-clad; grinning together at Disneyland, wearing mouse ears; and drinking fruit drinks together at frat parties. Through it all, I'd acknowledged in my own mind that Gina was attractive. But of course I'd been much too polite to say that to my new girlfriend, who had later become my wife.

Now, however, I couldn't disguise the shock and admiration that flooded me. It was all I could do to keep my tongue in my mouth.

Gina was gorgeous. Some girls blossom after college, I guess. Her fine, Italian features were framed by a magnificent mane of jet-black hair and punctuated with small horn-rimmed glasses that gave her the bookish look I find so sexy. With her, though, the look was more female executive than librarian. That fit with what I knew about Gina: she was an advertising analyst with an MBA, successful at her job and dedicated enough that even at twenty-eight she remained single.

But what floored me wasn't just her beautiful face, full kissable lips, or the rich glow of her olive-tan skin. It was the way her body looked under that tight, flattering business suit, all executive chic. Gina was *built*, the curves of her large breasts and full hips providing such a contrast to Brooke's wispy, slender form and angular bone structure. Both were incredibly sexy, but I guess I was so surprised to see Gina looking like such a sexpot that I couldn't hide my sudden, unexpected attraction.

Of course, Brooke and Gina had already planned my descent into depravity—without giving me the details, Brooke had assured me that plenty of attention had been paid to my deepest fantasies. That probably added something to the sexual tension between us.

"See?" said Brooke with a wicked smile. "I knew you'd think she was hot."

"Bubby!" shrieked Gina like a schoolgirl, using Brooke's college nickname. The two girls squealed as they rushed together, hugging excitedly. I couldn't help but notice the familiar way my wife let her hands rest on Gina's hips, nor the fact that they kissed on the lips—more than once.

"You must be Bob," said Gina, extending her hand.

"Gina," I said. "I've heard so much about you."

"Just the good stuff, I hope," said Gina.

Brooke hugged her close and kissed Gina on the side of the face. "With Gina," she cooed, "there's only good stuff to tell."

"Stop!" giggled Gina, and I reached for her bags.

For the next three days, I was all but forgotten as Gina and Brooke shared recollections of their wild and crazy college days. They stayed up late drinking wine and giggling, and I found myself sleeping alone. Brooke had taken the week off work, and while I was gone during the day the two of them cruised the city, which Gina had never visited before. Brooke showed Gina all of our favorite haunts, and by midweek I was feeling vaguely neglected.

Worse, though, Gina had proven to be pretty casual about making the house her own. She was sleeping on the couch, which created a few embarrassing moments. As I left for work early one morning, I saw that the blanket on the couch had slipped down below Gina's magnificent D-cup breasts, so different than Brooke's firm B-cups. I could see the outline of them clearly under the damp cotton sheet, her nipples firm and evident underneath. Her breasts moved up and down as she breathed softly in her sleep. I stopped dead in my tracks and stood there, staring, my cock stirring in my pants.

After a minute of that, Gina opened her eyes. "Hi," she said, her voice sexy and flirtatious. She didn't move to cover her breasts.

I looked away nervously and said, "Good morning," rather crisply. Then I hurried out the apartment door. As I stole a glance back at Gina, I saw that she was watching me, a smile on those full, lush Italian lips.

But nothing prepared me for what happened when I came home from work that Friday. As I walked in the front door of our apartment, leafing through a stack of bills from the mailbox, I stopped and listened.

There was moaning coming from the bedroom. I recognized Brooke's moans right away—after all, I'd made her utter them often enough. And it didn't take long for me to figure out that the second set of whimpers, moans, and grunts belonged to Gina.

I dropped the bills on the floor and walked softly to the door of the bedroom, which they'd left open.

There, sprawled on the bed, were my wife and her old friend, stark naked and locked passionately in a sixty-nine.

Gina was on top, her gorgeous ass deliciously facing me. Her legs were spread wide around my wife's face, and Brooke was eagerly eating her old friend's pussy while Gina humped just as eagerly up and down. Brooke's legs, too, were spread wide around Gina's face, and the old friend seemed to be giving as good as she got. Their hands roved all over each others' naked bodies, caressing as they ate each other out.

The room reeked of sex, telling me that they'd probably been at this all day. Their clothes lay scattered across the floor, as if they'd doffed them urgently, unable to wait to get each other into bed. *Our* bed. My wife was making love with a woman in our bed, right in front of my eyes.

I felt my cock quickly grow hard until it throbbed painfully. My cock swelled as quickly as my anger.

I don't know if I shifted or moved my feet, or if Brooke just sensed I was there. But she turned her head and looked back at me, her eyes wide in shock.

"Oh, god," she moaned. "Bob…"

I pulled the bedroom door shut and turned to leave the apartment.

Brooke caught up with me on the landing outside, still stark naked. She grabbed me and said, "I'm so sorry," trying to embrace me.

"You're standing here naked like a whore," I growled, my anger rising as I saw my wife's body glistening with the sweat Gina had coaxed out of her. "Like a fucking whore."

"I…I'm sorry," said Brooke, reddening more deeply. "She…she came on to me. I didn't mean for it to happen."

I felt my anger flaring, exploding into flames. "You bring a fucking slut into our house and then act surprised when she tumbles you into bed. Don't be a fucking idiot, Brooke."

"There's no need to be a bastard about it," snapped Brooke. She looked around, realizing that the neighbors could probably see her, standing there, naked. "When you're ready to talk about this, come back in the house."

She went back into the apartment. I chased after her and grabbed her shoulders from behind, pushing her onto the couch. She stumbled and fell, shrieking.

"Bob, you're being such a prick about this. It's really not that big a deal."

"Not that big a deal, is it?"

I could see Brooke's anger rising to match mine. "Gina

and I used to fool around in college," she said defensively. "When she came on to me, I figured it wouldn't be a problem if I did it for old times' sake."

I turned toward the bedroom, seeing Gina standing there in the doorway, her hands up on the jamb, her face twisted in a cruel smile. I let my eyes rove over her gorgeous body, admiring her full breasts with their firm nipples, now so erect from the passion of lovemaking. Her pussy was shaved smooth, her lips showing full and sex-swollen between her legs. There was a tattoo of a rose where her pubic hair had been shaved. Her face glistened with the juices of my wife's cunt.

I could smell sex, rich and ripe, the scent suffusing the apartment.

"It's true, Bob. I came on to her."

"You shut up," I said, pointing my finger at her. "If it's not a big deal, Brooke, then I'm going to fuck Gina, too."

Brooke's eyes went wide. "Wait—wait, don't be hasty, Bob, I—"

"I'm not being hasty," I said, turning to Gina. "What do you say, Gina? You want to save your best friend's marriage and spread those legs of yours?"

Gina smiled. "In an instant," she said. "Brooke tells me you've got a nice big cock."

"Come find out," I said, unbuckling my belt.

"Wait, wait," said Brooke. "Gina, don't do this."

Gina started toward me. When she put her arms around me, her naked body smelled moist and ripe with sweat. Brooke sat on the couch, stunned, staring at us as Gina pressed her lips to mine and wrapped her fingers around the bulge in my pants.

She turned to the seemingly horrified Brooke. It was

only later I realized that if I'd been watching more closely, I might have caught the look that passed between them—and Gina's wink.

But at that moment, all I saw was Gina's naked body, her tits pressed to me, her hand curving around my cock.

"Don't worry, Brooke," said Gina. "I have to do it. To save your marriage."

Brooke's expression changed, going from horror and anger to pleasure. She smiled.

"All right, Bob," she said. "Go ahead and fuck Gina. I'll watch." Brooke sat down on the couch, tucking her feet under her.

Gina unbuttoned my pants and worked the zipper down over my hard cock. She dropped to her knees, pulling my cock out.

The scent of the two women's naked bodies filled my nostrils. I was going to fuck Gina good, so good she'd scream. I was going to punish Brooke by making her watch me do Gina. It was a hateful thing to do, I knew, but my jealousy was driving me.

Brooke got off the couch, put her arms around me and kissed me fully on the lips. When her tongue slipped into my mouth, I could taste Gina's pussy, rich and tangy on my wife's mouth.

"I'm sorry, Bob," said Brooke when our lips separated. "I tried to be good. I was kind of hoping you'd make a move on her so I wouldn't have to feel guilty about it. Please tell me you're not mad."

"I am," I said.

At that moment Gina's lips closed around the head of my cock and began to slide up and down the erect shaft. I gasped and moaned softly as Brooke took my hand in hers and placed it on top of Gina's bobbing head. The two women guided me to the couch and sat me down; as Gina repositioned herself between my legs, I reached down and took hold of those magnificent tits I'd been spending the whole week fantasizing about touching. Brooke put her hand on mine and guided one of my thumbs to Gina's nipple. As I pinched gently her breathtaking face twisted in an expression of ecstasy, her nipples already sensitized from her long lovemaking session with my wife.

Brooke began to kiss me hungrily, our tongues mingling as she reached down to wrap her fingers around the base of my cock while Gina sucked the head. Brooke unbuttoned my shirt and began to suckle my nipples; I lay back on the couch.

"I'm still mad," I said. "Make it up to me."

"Oh, we will," said my wife mischievously, sliding down my body and joining Gina between my legs.

The two of them hungrily sucked on my cock. Gina licked her way to the top of my cockhead, swirling her tongue around the glans while Brooke took my balls into her mouth and lavished affection on them with her tongue. Gina's skilled fingers moved their way up to my nipples and played with them as she sucked me. Ever since I'd seen Gina at the airport, I'd longed to see her magnificent, full lips wrapped around my hard shaft. Her big, beautiful eyes looked up at me as she sucked my cock, telling me with their sparkle that she was enjoying this even more than I was.

Brooke came up for air from between my legs, leaving my balls sticky with her spittle as she massaged them with her hand. "Come to bed with us, Bob," she cooed. "We'll make it up to you, I promise."

Gina took one hand and Brooke took the other, and the two of them led me into our bedroom.

There's nothing like old friends, I decided, for keeping a marriage interesting.

Gina and Brooke kissed and fondled me as they slipped off my clothes. They pushed me naked onto the bed, which was still damp with their lovemaking. Gina got between my legs and ran her full lips up and down my cock again while Brooke settled down onto my face, leaning forward so she could enjoy my cock alongside her best friend. I greedily ate my wife's cunt. Brooke's moans mounted in volume with each stroke of my tongue on her pussy. She was gushing with arousal; I lapped up her juices as the two of them worked my cock. Soon Brooke's hips were grinding in time with my thrusts, and I knew she was close to coming.

"Roll over," sighed Brooke, lifting herself off my face.

"Why?" I asked.

Brooke looked down at me and giggled. "Just do it," she said. Gina's mouth came off my cock. I let them roll me onto my stomach. Brooke straddled my back. I felt her seize my wrists and push them into the black fabric straps I'd installed for the occasions when Brooke was in the mood for something kinky. I'd used them on her many times, strapping her spread-eagled to the bed before fucking her silly—but she'd never used them on me.

Gina was giving my ankles the same treatment, and before I knew it I was face down, my limbs spread, securely fastened.

"Hey," I said weakly. "You can't get at the good stuff if you tie me this way!"

Gina disappeared as Brooke slid down my body and began to kiss and nuzzle my neck, her legs spread around my ass.

"Oh, yes we can," she said, seizing my hair.

I could feel my cock throbbing against the sex-damp sheets, and it had just begun to dawn on me that I shouldn't have let these two women tie me up. "Hey," I growled. "I liked what we were doing before. Let me up."

Gina was beside the bed, handing my wife a ball gag. I opened my mouth to protest, and Brooke used that moment to stuff the ball gag into my mouth. I tried to spit it out, but she got the strap around the back of my head and pulled the buckle tight.

As I struggled against the bonds, it occurred to me that Gina had more than just the ball gag. I looked at her in horror. Gina was wearing a harness, into which was fitted a huge black dildo.

I tried to scream a protest, but the ball gag prevented it. I'd done a good job of installing the straps; I was bound and helpless. I heard the big, heavy bed frame creaking as I pulled against it in protest. I watched as Brooke leaned forward and wrapped her lips around the head of Gina's strapped-on cock. Her mouth glided eagerly up and down the shaft, the way she'd sucked my cock just a moment ago—the way she'd sucked my cock so many nights in the past.

Her lips came away from Gina's cock and strings of spit stretched from her mouth to the head.

"I bought this especially so Gina could fuck me with it," said Brooke. "But now I see she's got another task ahead of her. I'm never going to have the marriage I want unless we teach you a lesson, Bob. Don't you agree?"

I screamed a desperate protest behind the gag, but it only came out as a pathetic, muffled groan. Gina looked down at me and smiled, pretty as a peach, her beautiful lips still glistening from my cock and my wife's pussy. Then Brooke seized my hair and roughly pulled back my head. Gina slapped my face, hard, shocking me.

"Oooh," she said. "I like that." Her hand went to her cock and stroked it firmly. "It makes my dick hard."

Gina slapped me again, and I felt shame and humiliation wash over me. If they'd just take the gag out, I'd apologize for getting so angry—I'd beg Brooke to forgive me. Of course she could fool around with her old friend—I knew it didn't mean anything. I knew it was just for fun.

But they didn't take the gag out, and Brooke made it quite clear she had no intention of forgiving me.

Her hand tangled in my hair, she kept my head forced up, my face turned to Gina. Gina slapped me again, harder this time. And again. And again, harder, with the back of her hand, hitting me so hard my head spun. I felt sobs surging up in the back of my throat; Gina hit me again and again and again until I couldn't hold them down. My eyes filled with tears and sobs wracked my body.

"The little bitch starts to cry," Gina said mockingly. "He wasn't crying a minute ago when he told me I had to fuck him. Still want me to fuck you, Bob? Still want to make your wife's girlfriend put out for you?"

I couldn't answer; my eyes were blinded with tears and my whole body shook from the sobs that assaulted me. Brooke held my hair while Gina slapped me again, again, again, a dozen more times, harder each time as she wrenched my sobs out of me. I cried even harder when she pinched my cheeks between her thumb and forefinger and Brooke yanked my head back again. Gina hovered over me, pursed her lips, and let a great string of spit slip out from between them. The spit hit me, warm and wet, right on my cheek. Then she hawked, pursed her lips again, and spat, harder this time, a thick glob striking the bridge of my nose and oozing down.

"Oh, maybe he thinks if he cries enough, I'll go back to sucking his dick. Do you think I should go back to sucking his dick, Brooke?"

Brooke laughed, pulling my head back even more roughly. She hawked and spat, a big glob covering my face. I sobbed hysterically, my crying reduced to pathetic whimpers by the big gag in my mouth.

"I think he's the one who needs to suck dick," she said. "You shouldn't ever suck him again. I say we turn *him* into a cocksucker."

"Agreed," said Gina. "He obviously needs it."

With that, Brooke pulled the buckle of my ball gag and yanked it out of my mouth. I opened my mouth to scream, but before I could, the gag was replaced by Gina's cock. She shoved it into me so hard I couldn't help but swallow it; when the head spread open the tight entrance to my throat, I gagged, my stomach seizing up. Brooke held my head tight so I couldn't move. Gina forced her cock into my throat, not even caring that I was gagging and choking around it, my throat spasming around her shaft as she fucked my face.

"Not much of a deep-throater, is he?"

"He'll learn," said Brooke.

Gina mounted the bed, leaning against the headboard

and spreading her legs so she could hunker down and pump her hips, properly fucking my throat open wide. Brooke let go of my hair and Gina seized it, keeping my head in the right position, throat stretched out and straightened, for her to fuck it. Brooke climbed off of me and I heard a drawer opening; somehow, I knew what was coming. I heard the snap of a latex glove, the gurgling sound of lube being poured on it—the lube I used when I managed to talk Brooke into letting me fuck her in the ass.

"He's always been real big on anal sex," growled Brooke as she roughly pried open my cheeks, exposing my sensitive asshole. "I let him put it in me there, now and then, just to shut him up."

"Let's show him what it's like," said Gina, fucking my face more roughly than ever. She pinched my nose so I couldn't breathe, and I felt my lungs burning and my head pounding as she controlled my breath, only letting me gasp for air in the moments when her cock slid out of my throat.

Brooke slicked up her hand and I felt her fingers forcing their way into my ass. I squealed deep in my throat behind Gina's cock, but my wife wasn't interested in my protests.

"Look, the little piggy's still hard," she said, her free hand caressing my balls and stroking my shaft. "He's always wanted me to make him my bitch. Isn't that right, Bob?"

"Of course he has," Gina answered for me. "Why do you think he's such an asshole all the time? He knew if he was enough of a dick you'd finally snap—if he pushed hard enough you'd eventually flip him. He's been waiting for it all these years, baby."

"Oh, yeah, darling," sighed Brooke, stroking my cock.

"This is what you've always needed, isn't it? To be ass-fucked and raped in your throat?"

There was no answer possible—and Brooke didn't care.

She was pumping her fingers deep into my ass, moving them in circles so my ass stretched wider with each stroke. "That's two fingers," she said. "Now let's try three. Think you can take it, Bob?"

Gina was still pinching my nose and fucking my throat; there was no chance of my giving an answer. All I could do was lie there as my wife forced three fingers into my tight ass, stretching me open. She added more lube and chuckled.

"I think this little pig is going to take more. He's lucky I've got small hands. Here's four, darling. Open wide!"

With that, Brooke roughly shoved four fingers into my ass. I felt my sphincter stretching, my ass opened wide by her hand. I struggled against the bonds, but with all four limbs tied and Gina deep in my throat, there was little I could do. I felt more lube being poured between my cheeks, and my ass stretched further as my wife began to fuck it roughly with her hand.

"Think I can get my fist in here?" asked Brooke playfully. "I don't know, he's pretty tight-assed...."

"Oh, you can get it in there," laughed Gina. "If you shove hard enough."

I uttered a helpless groan of protest as I felt my ass stretching still more. Brooke forced her thumb into me, pointing her fingers just so, pumping in and out as she added still more lube, twisting her hand in rapidly widening circular motions as she forced my ass open.

"Get ready, darling," she cooed. "You're about to become

my fucking bitch. They say a man's never the same after he's been fucked in the ass. I bet it's even truer once he takes a fist in there."

I squealed, and Gina pinched my nose harder, ramming her cock deep into my throat to shut me up. Brooke shoved, and I felt my asshole stretching, protesting—and then giving way. Her hand sank into me and my whole body shuddered as I took her fist. I heard Brooke giggling, and Gina leaned over me so she could high-five Brooke's free hand. I felt lube splattering over my ass. Brooke pushed deeper into me, her fist filling me, sliding in, I thought, almost to the elbow.

"Sweet Jesus," said Brooke, stroking my cock. "He's still hard."

"Think he deserves a hand job?" asked Gina.

"Absolutely not. Untie his hands."

Gina's cock was still deep in my throat as she leaned over and pulled the buckles open. My hands hung limp, my arms stretched out to the side. I didn't move, afraid Brooke's hand in my ass would hurt me if I tried.

And afraid the pleasure flowing through me would stop.

I'd never been fucked in the ass before. I'd certainly never been fisted. And I'd never dreamed it could make my cock so fucking hard.

I felt Brooke's hand against the head of my cock. She used her fingers to guide the tight stretch of a condom down my shaft.

"Beat off, darling," she said. "Beat off with my fist in your ass."

I didn't move, just lay there, not believing what was happening as Gina slowly eased her cock out until the head rested between my lips. I couldn't move. I was frozen. It was one thing to be violated by my wife, forced to take her fist in my ass. It was the worst thing I could ever have dreamed of. But for her to know how much I was loving it, to know that I could stroke myself to orgasm while I was being so brutally taken—that was even worse.

"Come on, Bob," Gina cooed. "I know how much you love to stroke off. You think I don't know that you've been jerking off all week thinking about my tits? Come on. Stroke it."

"Don't play hard to get," said Brooke. "I know how much you love to jerk off. You think I don't know when you're doing it in the bathroom? When you sneak off to the garage and look at your *Hustlers?* Come on, Bob. Give up. I know you want to come. Do it."

My hand traveled slowly down my body and wrapped around my latex-sheathed cock. I moaned as I began to stroke it and Brooke and Gina both laughed. Then they started fucking me, harder than before, more brutally than ever. Gina's hips forced her cock down my throat again, making me gag and choke just as Brooke began to pound my ass, fucking her hand in and out of my asshole.

It only lasted a few seconds. Then I heard myself grunting rhythmically, my groans rendered staccato by the movement of the thick dildo in my throat. My cock pulsed and my entire body exploded with pleasure as I succumbed to the most intense orgasm of my life. My asshole clenched tight around my wife's fist as I came and came and came, filling the condom with what felt like gallons of come.

"That's a good boy," said Brooke, easing her hand back. She gently worked her hand around until she could slide it out of my ass. I heard the snap of her glove, and Brooke tossed the discarded latex across the room.

Gina pulled her cock out of my throat, and I gasped desperately for air, sobs attacking me again. Gina seized my hair and slapped my face again, harder—three times, four, half a dozen.

"It's no good crying, bitch," said Gina. "We know you loved it."

Gina came around the side of the bed as Brooke reached under me and gingerly unrolled the condom. I had thought my ordeal was over, but when Brooke climbed onto the bed in front of me, leaning against the headboard, I realized that it had just begun. Gina knelt behind me and guided the thick head of her cock to my fucked-open asshole. She drove into me so quickly that even my spread hole seized and clamped around it. But there was no resisting—Gina began to violently fuck my ass just as my wife clamped her legs around my face.

My arms still hung limp, untied, at my sides. My legs, however, were bound to the bed, forcing me open wide. There was nothing I could do to respond to Gina's violent, hateful invasion of my asshole.

Nothing, that is, except lift my hips and raise myself up to my knees, pushing myself onto her cock.

"Look, he's learned his lesson well," said Gina. "He's a little ass-bitch now. You can give it to him every night, and he'll fucking beg for it."

"It always happens," sighed Brooke as she grabbed my hair and forced my head back. "Once you ream them out, they're good little sluts for the rest of their lives. Now eat, darling."

I hadn't realized that she still had the condom—I'd thought she just didn't want me to make a mess when I came. But she had other things in mind, I realized as she forced the rubber ring of the condom's end between my lips and behind my teeth. She let go of my hair, roughly forced my mouth closed and, deftly using one hand, rolled the condom like a tube of toothpaste. I tasted my own come, felt it oozing into me, lukewarm goo from a rubber tube. I choked at first, not expecting the strong taste. But Brooke wouldn't take the condom away until she'd squeezed the last drop into my mouth.

"Swallow, dear," she said.

I swallowed, the taste overwhelming me and making even my cock-opened throat close tight. I managed to gulp it down with some difficulty, but as I finished, Gina slapped my ass hard, making me surge against her as she grabbed my hips and shoved me back onto her cock.

"*He's* fucking *me*," she laughed. "Come on, bitch, fuck yourself onto my cock."

She had my hips firmly between her hands, pulling me back to meet each thrust. I could have struggled now; I could have resisted. But I didn't; I let Gina's firm hands guide me up and down on her shaft.

As I felt my cock stirring, getting hard again.

"Ready for another go?" said Gina. "I think he's more virile than you let on." With that, she slapped my balls, and I gasped as my wife grabbed my hair. "I thought you said he didn't fuck you so good," said Gina.

"His cock's all right," she said. "But men are so obsessed with their pricks. It's their tongues that they should learn to use better."

Brooke shoved my face into her pussy and growled: "Show me how much you love me, bitch."

I began to tongue her cunt as Gina fucked my ass harder. She spanked my balls with every few thrusts, but even the seizing pain that rocketed through me with every rough blow on my nuts didn't stop my cock from pulsing to full erection. My tongue worked up and down as I suckled on my wife's clit, and she twisted her hand up tighter in my hair as she forced my face more roughly against her cunt. Her hips worked in time with my rhythm, and she began to moan as she neared her orgasm.

"I'm sorry," gasped Gina suddenly. "I've *got* to fucking come."

She got my ankles unstrapped in a moment, pushing me onto my side and twisting my lower body so she could get at my cock as I continue to eat Brooke's pussy. Gina wedged her thigh under my hip and straddled me, guiding my cock to her entrance. She slid onto my cock, her pussy wet and open as she leaned back, hanging partway off the bed. Her hand pressed tight against her clit and she rubbed fervently as my hips began to grind.

Brooke came loudly, moaning as she gripped my hair. I kept licking faster, just barely managing to coordinate my thrusts into Gina's pussy with my tongue against my wife's clit. When Brooke shuddered all over and finished coming, she slipped out from under me and pushed me hard onto Gina. Gina squirmed underneath me until she was spread, missionary-style, under my thrusting body, her hand still pushed between us working her clit.

Still quivering from her orgasm, Brooke curled up beside

me and nuzzled the back of my neck as I pumped into Gina. "Fuck her good, baby."

I was close to coming but Gina was even closer, and her hand came away from her clit just as she came, wrapping me in her arms and grabbing my ass to pull me roughly into her. I pounded faster and faster, feeling Gina's cunt tightening around my shaft as I thrust into it—and then she moaned loudly, the moan turning into a scream as her intense arousal drove her over the top.

I went rigid as my second orgasm ripped through me. I came in Gina's pussy, clutching her tight as Brooke stroked her hand down my sweat-sticky back. When I'd finished coming, Brooke put her arms around both of us and kissed Gina hard on the lips. Gina was so ruined from her orgasm that she could barely respond. As my soft cock slipped out of her she gasped.

"How's that for an anniversary celebration?" asked Gina. "As rough as you hoped?"

"Rougher than I'd imagined it could be," I said. "And everything I've ever wanted."

Brooke's hand found my ass and gingerly stroked the tender, moist hole, still oozing lube.

"It's true," she said. "There's nothing like old friends to keep a marriage interesting."

"You're lucky it's only five years," said Gina. "Just wait till your silver."

"I'm quivering in anticipation already."

Brooke playfully slapped my lube-slick ass.

"Just 'cause the scene's over, don't start getting smart," she said. "You're still my bitch."

I rolled off of Gina and took my wife in my arms.

"Of course I am, darling," I said.

"Don't get cute."

"Never," I said, snuggling close to her. "Never, ever."

Alice

M. CHRISTIAN

It started with the laundry—now how ironic is that?

It obviously was a kind of blind spot for Al. Ask him to take out the garbage, drive five hundred miles to help out a friend, weed the backyard, vacuum, even cook (he made a mean-ass clam chowder he was particularly proud of) and it would get done—so quick and so neat, in fact, that half the time jaws would drop and eyes would pop at how well done it was. No muss, no fuss: just a well-executed chore or perfectly performed task.

Just don't ask him to do the laundry. Domesticity might not be pretty, but the way Al faced stripping the bed, picking up crumpled clothing, hauling baskets downstairs, stuffing the washer, adding soap—the whole laundry procedure in fact—you'd think he'd been asked to give a sponge bath to Karl Malden.

Jeannine hadn't been bothered by it at first. "Your usual

breaking-in stuff," she thought to herself, said to some of her friends when they asked how their experiment in living together was progressing. "Nothing to worry a war crimes tribunal about."

Four months later it was, "Okay, it's starting to really bug me," she thought and said as she clenched her smooth hands into tight, white fists.

At six months she was wondering how to dispose of his body.

To be honest, he tried—and in many ways that simply made it worse. Huffing and puffing like a kid asked to eat his broccoli he'd make such a big production out of it that Jeannine didn't know whether to make him stand in a corner or give him a Golden Globe for overacting. Even when Al seemed to want to do it, earnestly "helping out around the house" on her birthday or when he'd done something spectacularly dumb and needed to do some housework Hail Marys, it didn't work out. Her favorite red dress, white shift, socks, the linen, dry clean onlys, even a suede jacket went in—and what came out went straight to Goodwill.

Despite Al's laundry issues, he and Jeannine had it pretty good: Al's underground comic, "The Snitch," was doing remarkably well—well enough that he didn't need a real job yet; Jeannine's store, Deco Mojo, was paying their rent and a little more; and unlike a lot of their friends, they'd been together for a little over a year with no sign of breakup or even nasty drama.

In all their time together, the months before and then after making the big leap of cohabitation, Jeannine and Al had a pretty cooperative relationship: some gives, some takes, fair play all the way around. Al did the shopping this week, Jeannine the next. This month Al paid the phone bill, next month Jeannine did. Except for the issue of the laundry, they kept everything fair and even between them.

That's not quite true, though. Everything was fair and even except for the laundry and one other place: the bedroom.

That's also not quite true—mainly because for Al and Jeannine the bedroom was only one of the places where they fucked around. The outdoors, you see, did it for Jeannine. The more out the better, especially when there was a real risk they'd get spotted by someone—extra especially when they could be spotted by more than just one someone. Parking garages, baseball games, movie theaters, hiking trails—they'd tried them all.

Al called it "eye-porn": the way Jeannine reacted to people looking was just like the way most guys reacted to looking at anything and anyone sexy. He loved it almost as much as Jeannine did: crawling up the fire escape to the roof, giggling and whispering like schoolgirls; laying out a blanket on gravel still warm from sunlight; a kiss, more kisses, clothes off, hands roaming, cock very hard, pussy very wet; fucking long and slow, then hard and fast knowing that either someone could be looking at them at any second or that hundreds—maybe thousands—were doing just that.

But what did Al like? "I'm not complaining, mind you," she thought and said to some of her friends when they'd first moved in. "Not at all."

Four months after that, "I just can't figure him out," was the order of the day.

At six she was wondering what terrible secret he was

hiding, what skeletons he had in his closet.

Then, one lazy Saturday afternoon—chores completed, laundry carefully ignored—they curled up together on their plush, painfully bright orange sofa (that Jeannine had never been able to sell) and started flipping through mail, stopping in the middle of the bills, the miscellaneous flyers, to glance at the Victoria's Secret catalog.

"Wow," Al said, brown eyes wide as Jeannine flipped through the glossy pages. "Pretty."

When they went to the museum—and after they snuck in a quick blow job in the French Impressionists—all Al said was "Nice." When they went to friends' gallery openings—and fucked ferociously in the grimy bathroom—all Al said was "Eh." "Good" was what Al called his world-renowned chowder, and how he described their sex life. In all their months Jeannine had never heard Al call anything else by that one word of praise. Until, that is, page seventy-nine of the Victoria's Secret catalog.

That night, after much thought, Jeannine smiled to herself. The next day, with the dreaded laundry, it was time for Al's skeleton to come out of the closet—and play.

"Perfect. Absolutely perfect. Or else," she said, obviously uncomfortable with even the idea of a threat—but even more obviously excited by it.

"Or else?" he said, as uncomfortable as she was with the threat—and just as excited.

"Or else you're going to be very intimate with some of my more intimates, Al. Do you get me?"

Al was speechless. But his face said what his voice couldn't.

"Good. Now, get it all done right, Al: fabric softener, the right temperature, no mixed colors, no running, nothing wrong. Perfect. No mistakes, Al." She cast him a cool glance. "I'm going out for a few hours—got some store stuff to take care of—and when I get back I expect the laundry to be done like it's never been done before."

Then she went out, with even a wider, more wicked, smile on her lips.

"Let me see," she said, four hours and some-odd minutes later. "Show me what you've got."

"Ah, sure—" Al said, nerves making him hesitate, stammer. "Sure thing, babe."

"Don't call me 'babe'—not yet, at any rate. Now show me. And this had better be good."

"Yes—" he started to say something that started with *b* but caught himself, substituting a quick "be right back," and a smile.

The first basket was full to overflowing with sheets, pillowcases, blankets, and towels. Jeannine tried to keep the smile off her face as he pulled out each neatly folded bundle. Creases almost made her giggle with joy, seams made her flash some pearly white teeth—but she fought to keep her face stony and firm.

"Now the next one," she said.

The next basket was packed with slacks, jeans, blouses, socks, boxers, bras, shirts, and panties. Al may have screwed up every other attempt at laundry, but this time he gleamed, shone, sparkled, was absolutely spotless. She may have barely kept the smile from her face before, but now it took every ounce of her control to keep from laughing and giving him a big hug—and the laundry had nothing to do with it.

But she had to find something wrong. That was the game, after all. "What's this?" she said, holding up a pair of panties.

"Um, er—it's your…panties."

"That's right, it's my favorite pair: soft, pearlescent, pure white with the frilly waistband and the tiny blue flower right in the middle. Right there. See the flower? But there's something about this flower, Al—something very, very bad."

Al swallowed hard but didn't say anything.

"You see, Al, my favorite pair of silky panties has four little green leaves next to that sweet little flower. Four. Not two, not three, not five—four. Now, Al, I want you to take these and tell me how many little green leaves there are next to that so-sweet little flower."

Al took the panties in suddenly moist hands, turned them carefully until the little flower was turned toward him. Just as Jeannine had never heard Al use the word *pretty* before—not at the museum, not in a gallery—she'd never really seen him hold something reverently before.

"Three," Al said, glancing up from the panties to look her in the face. His eyes were wide and gently moist.

"That's right, Al. Three. Not four—three. One of my leaves is missing. That's not a good thing. Not a good thing at all. I asked you to do something and you didn't do it. I'm afraid, Al, that you'll have to be punished."

Al's face lit with a soft smile. "I understand." He seemed to want to add something else (Ma'am, Sir, Mistress, something like that) but didn't know what to say—yet.

"Good. Now strip."

Al's smile grew, took on a sweetness and a subtle *thank*

you, and he did as he was told.

Next to one of the baskets went his hurriedly shed shirt, shoes, pants, socks, and underwear, until he stood in front of her, tall and lean, all long bones and tight muscles, and very, very hard.

Jeannine looked at his gently bobbing cock. It took a lot of control not to reach out and stroke it, suck it. "Very good," she said, her voice catching in her throat. She doubted she'd ever seen him as hard. "Very, very good. Now, Al—" she tossed him the sheer panties "—put these on."

At first Al didn't do anything. He just stood in front of her, very hard, with a strange expression on his face. Later, when she had time to really think about it, Jeannine would realize that among the emotions that were zapping around inside her boyfriend's mind—desire, suspicion, shame, fear, to name a few—the one that finally won out, that made him reach down and put one foot, then the other, into the satin undies and slowly, sensually draw them up his body, was relief.

"Very nice," Jeannine said, surprising herself at her own sincerity. He really did look...not pretty, but definitely very sexy: his very hard cock tented the white material like he was trying to shoplift a javelin, and the sheer material was already growing damp at the end with pearly pre-come. Again, it took all of Jeannine's control not to just lick the end, taste the salty bitterness. "Very sexy, Al—no, that's not right. You're not really Al, are you? Not right now."

Al hung his head slightly, pulled his elbows and knees in, shrinking, getting younger, the rough and tumble Al fading away as Jeannine watched.

"Alice?" Jeannine said, the inspiration like a small shock.

"Your name is Alice. Isn't that right…Alice?"

Al—no, because her boyfriend was gone; Alice, her girlfriend with the white satin panties, very big clit, and very small boobs, nodded slowly, happily.

"You're very pretty, Alice, in nothing but your white panties. Very sexy. Do you feel sexy, Alice?"

Alice smiled, radiantly, saying, but not with words: *Yes, very much so.*

"Turn around, Alice. Show me your sexy little body. Show me what you've got, slut."

Alice chewed a thumbnail, eyes wide and moist.

"Do it, Alice—or do you want me to be upset?" Jeannine wanted to laugh, to cry at how excited they both seemed to feel. It wasn't a game she'd played before—or would ever have thought about playing with Al—but with Alice it seemed right, natural, and most of all, way too much fun.

Alice's eyes grew even wider. Then, slowly, shyly, she turned around, giving Jeannine a hesitant view of her boyish body.

"Very sexy," Jeannine said, suddenly aware of her own wetness. "I really like you in my panties. In fact, I think you look even better in my panties than I do. They're yours now."

"T—thank you," Alice said; even her voice was soft and almost innocent.

Jeannine leaned forward and grabbed hold of Alice's huge clit in a powerful grip. Alice was startled, but Jeannine hung on and wouldn't let her pull away. "You forget your place…Alice. Do you want me to be displeased?"

"N—no," stammered Alice, hands falling to Jeannine's. Touching, but not trying to pull them away.

"'No,' what? Who am I, Alice? What do you call me?"

Alice's face burned bright red. Her lips quavered but no words came out.

"Say it, Alice—or I put you to bed without any supper."

"Mistress…" whispered Alice. Then, with a bit more force: "Yes, Mistress," like a weight had been lifted.

"That's right. I'm your Mistress. Don't you forget it, either." She let go of Alice's clit. The thin girl took a half step back in response.

"No—no, Mistress, I won't forget," Alice said, composing herself.

"You'd better not." Jeannine reached out and ran her fingers up the length of Alice's very hard, rhythmically flexing clit. "So beautiful—" she said, almost whispering. Shaking her head slowly, as if to clear it, she said in a louder voice, "Now then, slut. Where were we? Oh, yes, that's right. You were giving me a show. I like a good show."

Jeannine leaned back as if to inspect her new plaything. "Why don't you show me how hard that clit of yours really is. Rub it for me, stroke it through your new panties. Do it. Do it now."

"Yes, Mistress," Alice said, her voice honey and all manner of sweetness. Palm down, she dropped one hand to the front of her panties and slowly started to rub herself.

"That's it," Jeannine said, gently parting her own legs in response, as if Alice's clit was somehow connected directly to her own. "That's it."

"Thank you, Mistress, " Alice said, her eyes glazing over in pleasure. As she rubbed, stroked herself, the front of her panties got wetter and wetter. Soon, the pale material was almost transparent, giving Jeannine a perfect view of the thin girl's monstrous clit. "Thank you…" said Alice.

"Oh, yes, you slut. You love this, don't you, slut? You love it, being the nasty little girl, putting on a show just for me. Yeah, that's it; rub it, rub that sweet clit for me. Make those panties nice and hot and wet and sticky. Stroke it for me, stroke it…."

Alice bit down on her lip, her breath coming in shorter and shorter hisses until, finally, she didn't make any sound at all but her body tensed as if a kind of wonderful voltage slammed through her. Rigid, locked tight in a shuddering orgasm, the front of her panties were suddenly soaked with her sticky juices.

In a barely controlled fall, Alice dropped down first to her knees and then face-first onto the carpet. She lay there for a long time, her body quivering and quaking with release, breaths now heavy and slow.

"Very, very good, slut," Jeannine said reaching up under her simple skirt to hook a thumb into the waistband of her own everyday panties. "That was quite a show. Quite a *nice* show. I'm very impressed." The panties came off, soaked through. She tossed them aside. "In fact, come here, Alice," she said, her voice a husky whisper, "and taste how impressed I am."

Slowly, weak only in body, Alice got to her knees and moved over to Jeannine until her face was parallel with Jeannine's downy pubic hairs.

Now it was Jeannine's turn to really smile, as the game got even better for her. Leaning down, she parted her plush lips, giving Alice a view of her very wet folds and pulsing clit.

"Taste," she managed to get out before her voice got completely caught in her throat.

Alice did. Alice did, indeed. Nuzzling up between Jeannine's strong thighs she flicked her tongue over her clit. Hard and fast, slow and soft, Alice licked. Jeannine, standing above her but at that instant miles way, moaned and bucked, dipped and swayed in response.

Finally, the pressure that Alice had been applying to her peaked and she cried—her version short and sharp and loud compared to Alice's almost silent and long one—and slid down to sit, hard, on the floor at Alice's feet.

While her body was still working, she threw her hands around Alice, her girlfriend, and Al, her boyfriend, and cried hot tears of pleasure and wonderful discovery.

Some stories really do have happy endings. Al's comic work continued to do well, receiving both critical and financial success. Jeannine's store became a hallmark of the neighborhood. Al and Jeannine, and Alice and Jeannine were very happy together—and their whites were whiter, their colors brighter than ever before.

Full Body

Simon Torrio

After a long soak in the tub, I'm ready for a hand job. I climb out of the tub, towel off, and pass from the small hot tub area into the massage room. Even though there's a door between them, the massage room still stinks of chlorine; it also smells vaguely of male sweat and more than a hint of mildew. I stretch out on the massage table with its threadbare sheet, dark blue so the stains won't show. I pull the second sheet over my hard-on and flip the switch next to the table.

You come into the massage room a moment later. I look you up and down approvingly. You're wearing skintight red hot pants, very low cut, top button unbuttoned. Your almost see-through white halter shows off the curves of your large breasts, and the slight peaks of your nipples stretch the fabric. Your long legs are perched on gold high heels. The gold doesn't quite match your shoulder-length hair, a badly-bleached shade of yellow slightly messed up from the last client—I guess.

"Hi, I'm April," you tell me, smiling.

"Hi, April," I say, smiling at you as I let my eyes linger over your tits and the top button of your hot pants where the low waist shows off your hips. Your tattoo of stylized green and black ivy hovers around the top of the shorts, accenting the glint of your navel ring. I wonder if I'll find anything else pierced down below.

You purse your full, garishly red lips, making them as kissable as possible. "A rubdown is included in the price," you tell me, businesslike. "But if you'd like me to take off my top, it's another fifty dollars."

"How much for full service?" I ask.

"We don't do that here," you say, as if you've fielded the question a thousand times. "For me to take off my shorts, it's seventy-five, and to see me totally nude it's a hundred."

"And how much is it to fuck you?" I ask.

"That's not allowed," you say. "Would you like me as I am, topless, shorts off, or fully nude?"

"That depends," I say. "What are you wearing under those shorts?"

"Why don't you pay me the seventy-five, and you can decide if you want the shorts off after you see."

"What if I want to fuck you?"

"I don't do that," you say irritably.

I sigh in disappointment. "The money's on the table," I tell you. "That should be enough to let me fuck you."

"I told you," you say. "We don't do that here."

"Oral? I'd love to fuck that pretty mouth of yours," I tell you, staring hungrily.

"No, I don't do that, either."

"Then at least give me a hand job," I smile at you innocently. "That's not too much to ask, is it?"

"That's not allowed either," you tell me. "But if you'd like to finish yourself, that's all right."

"Take off your clothes," I tell you.

You prance over to the tip table, tottering in your tacky high heels. You pick up the wad of money and count the twenty-dollar bills.

"This is way too much," you say.

"I figured that'd be enough if I wanted to fuck you."

"I told you, I don't do that," you say. "But this'll get you fully nude. And full body."

"Full body?"

"I'll climb on top of you," you say. "Only while you're lying on your stomach."

"And a hand job?"

You look down, guiltily. Your eyes flicker up and linger for a moment on the bulge under the sheet, the hard-on I've had since before you walked in the room.

"Yeah," you say. "I can give you a release at the end."

"Sold," I tell you, and you roll the three hundred dollars up tight and put it in the pocket of your shorts. You come over to me and turn your back, leaning back to show me the tie of your white halter top.

"Will you untie me?" you ask.

I quickly curl my arm around you, move my hand up your belly and cup your breast, squeezing the nipple gently. It's very hard.

"I'd rather rip it off of you," I say.

"That's not allowed," you say, pulling away. You reach

behind your back and untie the halter. Stretched tight, it pops forward around your tits. As I watch, you unfasten the tie at the back of your neck and let the halter slip away from your breasts. They're big and round, gorgeous, with nipples that are much harder than when you walked in.

"Nice," I say. "Now the shorts."

You unbutton your fly and wriggle out of your shorts, sliding them down your long legs to show me perfect hips and a crotch covered only by a tiny, cheap red lace thong. You fold the halter and shorts together and place them on the table. You stand there for me to look at, and I smile.

"What are you waiting for?" I ask you. "Lose the thong."

You peel the thong away from your pussy, and I discover that you're shaved—smooth. You've got a ring in your clit and a heart-shaped tattoo just above your pussy, in the shaved patch. The name across it says *DADDY*. I can smell your cunt in the small room, musky and sweet. My cock pulses under the sheet.

"Roll over," you say, edging toward the table.

"I'd rather have you climb on top of me this way," I say, pulling down the sheet and revealing my hard-on.

"Uh-uh." You shake your head. "Roll over."

Grudgingly, I toss the top sheet on the floor and roll onto my stomach. My hard-on presses painfully against the padded massage table. You climb on my back and straddle me, your pussy wet against the small of my back. From the moment it touches me I feel the energy throbbing into my body, electric. I've got to fuck you if it's the last thing I do.

You drape your body over mine and start to brush your big tits down my back as you grind your hips against me, rubbing your pussy against the curve of my ass. I moan softly as you dry-fuck me and stroke your erect nipples over my shoulders. As you bend forward, drawing your breasts down my back, I feel your breath hot against the back of my neck. You move down and straddle the back of one thigh, your cunt rubbing against me. Your hands trace patterns down my sides, and your breasts shudder back and forth on my skin. Your pussy rubs more firmly against the back of my thigh. I can feel the hard prick of the small ring in your clit. I can also feel your pussy getting wetter, sliding juicy up the back of my leg, leaving a cool trail of moisture. The last trick's lube leaking out of you—or a hooker getting turned on? The way your breathing changes—quicker, almost imperceptibly—could be an act, but the hardness of your nipples couldn't be. It's too warm in here to explain their firmness, but not warm enough to make either of us sweat, to explain the moisture between your legs. You press your lips to the back of my neck, trailing your tongue along it—but it's practiced, businesslike. You lift yourself onto your hands and knees above me, and I can feel the trickle of wetness you left on the back of my leg, close to my ass. You start to kiss your way down my back, your tongue barely touching me.

I do it fast—fast enough that you don't see it's happening until I've rolled almost all the way over. By that time I've dislodged you from above me; you've lost your balance and you would have fallen if my arm hadn't shot out and curved around your waist, catching you. When I pull you onto me, I've rolled over and your legs are spread around my cock, your wet pussy an inch away from it.

Your eyes are wide, your lips parted. You're breathing quickly.

"There's another two hundred in my wallet," I tell you. "Why don't you go get it?"

You shake your head. "It's not allowed." You start to squirm away, weakly.

My hands hold your hips, and I pull you down onto me, my cockhead nudging between your lips. Your muscles tense and you try to pull off of me, but your heart's not in it. You're propped on your elbows, your face close to mine. "Three hundred," I say, and kiss you on the lips. My tongue forces its way into your mouth and I feel your tongue stud. Your tongue stays limp, loose, slack, helpless as I savage it with mine. I lift my hips a little and the head of my cock presses moist with pre-come against your clit.

"Four hundred," I tell you, and reach around behind you to get hold of my cock, putting it in just the right position at the entrance to your cunt.

Your eyes go wide, looking into mine. I want you to nod, but you can't. You just look, breathing hard, not saying no, not saying yes.

"Go get the money," I tell you. "It's in my pants pocket."

You shake your head weakly. "After," you say, your voice hoarse. "We'll do it after."

I pull you down onto me, and you groan as my cock goes into you. Your pussy is dripping wet through, and it slides down so easily over my cock that I plunge all the way into you in an instant. I hold you there, grinding my hips up against you, feeling my pubic bone against your clit.

Then I kiss you again, harder this time, forcing my tongue against yours, deep, taking your mouth as I use your pussy.

Your hips start to move; you lift yourself up on my cock

and slide back down, gasping as you do. You start to fuck me. I can feel the thick swelling of your pussy against the head of my cock, and you work yourself onto me more rhythmically as your pussy gets tighter, swelling with blood, filling with lust. You claw at the massage table, whimpering as you fuck yourself onto my cock. It isn't long before I feel your body go tense.

"I'm—going—to—"

You're not faking it, either—not unless you're very, very good. Your hips pump eagerly until your cunt begins to contract around my shaft, and then your whole naked body shudders. You stop thrusting and I take up the motion, pounding up into you, pumping deep into you with every circling motion of my hips. You come hard on my cock, trying hard to stifle your moan so the other clients in the nearby rooms won't hear—but there's little you can do to keep yourself from crying out. You moan so loud you hurt my ears.

When you're finished coming, your body is limp. I lift you up and slide out from under you, repositioning you on the massage table. You let me do whatever I want, lying there like a rag doll as I prop you up on just your knees, your arms hanging useless over the sides of the table and your face and tits pressed into the dark sheet. I spread your legs wider and enter you from behind, and you gasp as I do. I start to fuck you hard, pounding into you, your beautiful ass spread out under me. I lick my thumb and slide it between your cheeks, nuzzling your asshole. I hear a quick, surprised gasp, like you're going to say "No," but you don't. Instead, your gasp becomes a low moan as I work my spit-slick thumb into your ass. I slide it in deep, feeling my thumb against my cock as I fuck you faster. Your hips are lifted high, your ass thrust up toward me, and you're barely moving at first. But as my cock slides into you more rapidly, you start to grind against me. You start to fuck me back, moaning even louder than when you came.

Your ass is so tight around my thumb, I can't resist it. I spy the bottle of massage oil next to the table, crusted and clouded like it's never been used. I snatch it up with my free hand and slide my thumb out enough to drizzle a stream of oil between your cheeks. Rubbing it in, I slide my thumb into you more easily, then add more oil.

"Wh—what are you doing?" you ask between moans.

"I'm fucking you in the ass," I say, easing my cock out of your pussy and moving it up to the tight bud of your rear opening.

"G—Greek's—" you gasp, unable to finish the sentence as I nuzzle my cockhead against the entrance to your ass. "Greek's—um—Greek costs—" You grope after the words, like you're desperately trying to think of an appropriate price, but you can't find one—and I know you've never done it before. I push my cockhead into your ass, and it feels tighter than anything I've ever fucked. I go slow at first, listening to your little squeals as you feel your ass acclimating to the bulk of my cock. Slowly you relax and I slide my cock deeper, until you're wriggling against the table, fully impaled on my cock. And moaning.

I lean forward hard against your body, forcing your hips down and your legs wide. I start to fuck your ass and I feel the tickle of your fingers against my balls. I realize you've slipped your hands between your legs and you're urgently rubbing your clit. Your moans rise in volume as I pound into your asshole. Within minutes I feel you thrashing against me, your hand quickening. I take over, reaching under you and pushing my hand over yours, forcing you to rub your clit harder as I drive into your ass with new fury. When you come, your ass clenches so tight it almost forces me out, and I have to fuck you harder, almost violently shoving it into your ass to keep it sliding in as you come in great shuddering spasms. Then I come, too, as your climax intensifies and you start to lose it, shaking back and forth under me, lifting your ass to take deeper thrusts as I shoot my come deep inside you. When I'm finished, you lie there, panting with exhaustion.

I stretch and slide out of your ass, climbing off the table. I leave you there, ass upturned and opened wide, as I get dressed. You moan softly, eyes wide, staring at me but unseeing. Your hand is still pressed against your clit.

Before I leave, I take out my wallet and count out four bills.

"Four hundred dollars," I say, and leave it on the table. "Thanks for the massage."

I leave the room without kissing you good-bye.

Outside, I pass another couple and wink at them under the big sign that says *NO SEXUAL ACTIVITY*. The woman smiles at me; the guy looks away.

As I walk down the long line of doors, I can hear the occasional moan in the rooms beyond. I know this place is a poorly-kept call girl's secret; more outcalls happen here than in any hotel in town, if only because they rent by the hour and they don't offer full-body massages—thus eliminating the chance of unexpected competition after the fact.

That's why you and I picked this place; a friend of ours who works as an escort tipped us off that it's a place where you can make as much noise as you want—and no one will bother you. But today I think you pushed your luck on even that rule, with your screaming climax as I fucked your ass. Normally it wouldn't matter, except I think we'll be coming back here a lot.

I leave a twenty for the towel girl and wait for you in the lobby. When you come out, wearing jeans and a T-shirt, you have that nervous glow about you that says, "I just got laid." I wonder if I have the same look.

You smile at me and we head for the car.

In the Back of Raquel

P. S. HAVEN

It was after midnight when I arrived. I checked the name Trinh had scrawled on the napkin against the sign on the façade and then parked Raquel under a streetlight and joined the steady stream disappearing into the club. The music was loud and hypnotic, and I had to ask twice of the girl behind the ticket counter what the cover was.

"Thirteen," she yelled, and I peeled the bills from my money clip and stepped into the smoky neon haze, surrounded suddenly by the flash of naked skin as skirts fluttered and raised, revealing sweaty thongs and hips gyrating to the relentless electronic grind of the music. I moved quickly, hugging the wall as I avoided the dancing, surging throng, navigated the rows of tables along the outskirts of the dance floor, and finally slipped behind the railing that separated the liquor bar from the rest of the club.

I saw Elisa, standing at the bar and sipping something blue, obviously alone despite the fact that she was surrounded. She was wearing the dress, despite her protestation that it fit better last year. It was black, of course, satin, no larger than a pillowcase, baring her entire back, her skin as pale as moths' wings. It was short, sheer, and sleek, the hem floating about her thighs, the banded tops of her coffee-colored nylons just visible. Elisa saw me in the mirror over the bar and watched me as I made my way toward her, a slow smile creeping across her face as she smoothed the satin to her body with her palms, her hips swaying, her legs long and slender in five-inch patent spikes. Perfect. She returned to her drink as I approached.

"Sorry I'm late."

"You're not," Elisa said. "Late, that is."

"How long have you been here?"

"Not long," she lied. Elisa sipped from her drink and then leaned into me, kissing me softly, leaving behind an intoxicating scent of alcohol and perfume. She gestured with her drink toward the crowd outside the bar. "They have a table. Let's go."

Elisa and I made our way around the dance floor, one of her hands tucked into my arm, the other holding her drink carefully away from stray dancers. Trinh and Trey were seated at a small table near the DJ's booth, and Trinh spotted us and waved with a flick of her tiny wrist. Trey rose as we approached, extending his hand. "Good to see you again," he said, a little louder than he had to.

"You remember Trey," Trinh told me. I nodded and smiled, and took Trey's hand and shook it.

"Hope I haven't kept you waiting," I said to Trey.

"Not at all," Trey smiled and everything about him seemed to almost shine; his blond hair, his golden skin, his silk shirt, even his fucking teeth. We sat and a girl with pink hair instantly appeared to take our drink order. Elisa showed the girl her blue drink and I ordered a beer, as did Trey. Trinh told the girl she wanted a cosmo and got only a confused look.

"A cosmo*politan*," Trinh snarled, leaving the girl to walk away muttering "cunt" to herself, not quite loud enough for Trinh to hear her over the music's incessant throb. Trinh lit a thin, exotic-looking cigarette and smiled, either unaware or unconcerned she had just been insulted.

Our drinks arrived mercifully fast and after tasting hers, Trinh let out a little laugh and said to Trey and me, "Maybe you two should get to know each other." I drank my beer and listened to him convincingly enough, nodding and responding when appropriate, and based on very little conversation, I decided that we had absolutely nothing in common except Elisa. Trey began to tell me how lucky I was to be married to such a beautiful, intelligent woman and I could see Elisa blush.

"Let's dance," Elisa abruptly interjected. She was up and ready, pulling me by my wrist, tugging at me like a child, her voice insistent. I pantomimed my protest, exaggerating my reluctance as I held fast in my chair until Elisa took Trey by the hand, and said, smiling, "You, then." Trey needed no encouragement and Elisa led him onto the floor, checking over her shoulder as the pulsing crowd absorbed them, making sure I was watching. I was.

As Trinh and I watched, Elisa and Trey began to dance, their bodies pressing into each other as they moved to the music, Elisa's little dress twitching about her thighs. Watching them dance, it would've been easy to mistake them for lovers, Trey's hands gliding onto Elisa's naked back. But they weren't lovers. Not yet, anyhow. I watched his hands slowly move around her waist before sliding down onto the swaying curves of her hips, clutching at the smooth fabric of her dress, pulling it taut across her ass. Her buttocks were soft and full, and for just an instant Trey's hands seem to hold them before moving quickly up her back, letting her dress fall free. For a moment, the bodies surrounding them parted and Elisa's eyes met mine. In them I could see that she knew I was right, that what I had been telling her all along was true: she was still sexy. She was still desirable. And Trey knew it, too. And there was suddenly an unfamiliar fluttering in my stomach and for a moment I thought it was jealousy.

"So," Trinh said abruptly, starting one of her sentences that come out of nowhere and disappear just as fast. I waited as she drained her cosmopolitan before gesturing toward Elisa and Trey with her emptied glass. "What do you think?" I looked back at Elisa, watched her smiling up at Trey, her arms slung around his neck, causing her dress to rise on her hips. Trinh stabbed her cigarette into the glass ashtray on the table, the butt rimmed with her maroon lipstick, and before I realized it, she had slipped silently into Elisa's vacant seat next to me. "Is he attractive? Do you like him?"

"All I want is to see her fuck him. Then I can get on with my life."

"He's only twenty-two," Trinh said, almost whispering, as if trying to keep it a secret. "And he's hung like a fucking *horse*." The pink-haired girl had lit at the table behind us, and Trinh turned to show the girl her empty glass, and I took a good look at Trinh for the first time since I'd arrived. She was Vietnamese, I finally decided, pretty and quite young, even more so than I had originally thought. Her hand was on my leg and I looked down at it and beyond to her crossed legs, long and bronze, naked almost to her waist, her tiny black skirt stretched across her lap, and she tugged at it once to let me know she knew I was looking. Then she said, "Are you sure you want to go through with this?"

I looked at Trinh and for a moment I was tempted to tell her everything. For a moment I wanted to tell her how Elisa and I used to be when we were first married, when we couldn't get enough of each other, before we became distracted by our careers, our schedules, our money. I wanted to tell her how mortgages, a kid, and fourteen years had all conspired to somehow, inexplicably, turn us into old married people. But only for a moment.

Before I had to give Trinh an answer the drink girl came back and dropped off Trinh's cosmopolitan as well as another blue drink for Elisa and two more beers. I looked again for Elisa, and for a moment couldn't find her, then she and Trey suddenly appeared at the table and sat in the two seats across from Trinh and me. Elisa smiled at me and I could see her chest rising, her skin glistening with sweat. They began their fresh drinks in unison.

"You two look good together," Trinh said to them, and then to me, "Didn't they?" She was right, but I couldn't answer before she said to Trey, "He likes to watch."

"Really?" Trey said, almost laughing.

"What about you, Trey?" Trinh went on. "You like watching?"

"I like *doing*."

"Sounds like you two are perfect for each other," Trinh laughed, pointing at me with her glass and at Trey with her finger. Trey suddenly stood and announced to the table (and anyone else within earshot) that he had to take a piss, then disappeared into the darkness as Elisa watched.

When he was out of sight, Elisa turned to me and said, simply, "Well?"

And then Trinh: "What are you afraid of?"

It was a challenge, not a question. I understood this, but I had an answer nonetheless. More than anything, I was afraid of regret. Regretting doing this. Regretting *not* doing this. What if Elisa hated herself for doing this? What if she hated *me* for letting her? What do you do when fantasy and reality lie too far apart? I looked at my wife, looked for the answers, and in her eyes I could see that it was now or never, too close to the latter. I could see that she was ready, for the first and only time, maybe, to let this happen, and I knew that I had only that moment to make my decision.

"Do you want to or not?" Elisa asked me.

Of course I wanted to. For as long as I had been married to Elisa this had been my deepest desire, my most pervasive fantasy. But it had always been just that: *a fantasy*, things said in the heat of the moment, with the understanding that we never really intended to act upon them. Until now. I had no way of knowing what would happen if I said yes—I hadn't even known Trey before tonight—and somehow that excited me even more.

Before I could say anything, Elisa saw Trey returning. "Do you love me?" she said quickly.

"Yes."

"Do you trust me?"

"Of course," I said.

"Then trust me, you'll love this."

"1967 Shelby Mustang GT500," Trinh suddenly began to recite as we approached Raquel. "428-cubic-inch engine, two Holley 600 cfm four-barrel carburetors. 355 horsepower." Trinh ran her fingers down Raquel's fender and across the chrome Cobra badge. "Only two-thousand-forty-seven ever made."

"Two-thousand-forty-eight," I said.

As I produced the keys from my front pocket Trinh asked, "May I?" She was smiling, her hand outstretched. Trinh could sense my hesitation and said, "Not a scratch. I promise."

Any other night, any other circumstances, I wouldn't have even considered it, and I think Elisa was as surprised as I was when I handed over the keys and turned to quietly ask her, "Are you sure you're okay with this?" She nodded, but it wasn't enough for me. "You don't have to do this," I said.

"Do you want me to?" Elisa said.

"I...yes."

"Then I have to," Elisa said, and then, as Trinh watched and waited, kissed me. It was a perfunctory, almost calculated kiss. Almost like the kiss she gave me when we got married, the "you-may-now-kiss-the-bride" kiss. The kind of kiss that was meant more for the people watching than the person receiving it. And I thought, then, of the vows we'd made before giving each other that kiss. Vows to love, cherish, and obey. And how, in some strange way, by letting happen what was surely about to, Elisa was honoring those vows.

Trinh told Elisa she would be riding in the back and Elisa obediently climbed in, followed immediately by Trey, his distended cock straining conspicuously against the front of his pants as if following Elisa of its own free will. Trinh slid behind the wheel, tugging at her skirt as she sat, and I walked around Raquel to the passenger side, Elisa watching me through the back glass, her eyes bright, childlike with anticipation.

I got in and Trinh hit the starter, Raquel rumbled to life, and we moved through the maze of one-way downtown streets, starting and stopping at traffic lights until the road opened up. Trinh wound her way through the gears, redlining every one as we got out on the highway, and I realized as I watched her that I had never been in Raquel's passenger seat before, had never let anyone else drive her. And I started to notice things that I could only see from this point of view: the green glow the gauges cast on the driver's face; the relative positions of the clutch and accelerator, the gearshift and the wheel; and how Trinh was almost too slight to use all four at the same time.

Trinh adjusted the rearview mirror until she and I could see Elisa and Trey in the blue shadows of the backseat, intermittent bands of light sweeping across their faces as we passed under streetlights. Trinh lit a cigarette, its red glow dancing across the interior of the car, and she almost sighed as she exhaled the thick smoke. "Do you like sucking cock, Elisa?" she said suddenly as I watched the speedometer creep past eighty.

"What?" Elisa said, her voice barely loud enough to hear.

"You heard me," Trinh told her. "Simple question, yes or no?"

"I…" Elisa began tentatively. "Yes."

Trinh turned to look at Elisa over her shoulder. "So suck Trey's cock. Right now." Elisa looked for me in the mirror, and Trinh said, "It's okay. He doesn't mind," then turning to me she added, "Do you?" Trinh inhaled the last of her cigarette and cracked the window, the wind rushing in cold and loud, and flicked the butt outside before sealing the window again.

"I don't mind," I heard myself say. Trinh lit another cigarette and watched me as I watched Elisa in the mirror. "Drive faster," I told Trinh, and she did.

As I watched, Elisa dropped from view and I could see Trey settling into the seat, sliding down a little; draping one arm across the back of the seat, the other over my wife. Trinh smiled, as if relieved, or happy, maybe, that she didn't have to talk Elisa into it. Over the drone of the engine I could hear the faint clinking sound of Trey's belt being unbuckled. Then I could hear the wet noise of Elisa's mouth, and by the look on Trey's face I knew that Elisa had his cock out and had begun.

I stared into the mirror, straining to see in the darkness, and I could make out the dark shape of Elisa's body curling up in the seat next to Trey, her head moving in his lap. "Drive faster," I said again, glancing over at the speedometer, the needle arcing past one hundred. In the mirror I could see Trey, breathing deeply, sinking further into the seat, relaxing, both arms now slung across the back of the seat. Trey's eyes met mine, and I stared helplessly at him, unable to turn away; his eyes were white slits, half hidden in the shadows, and I suddenly had the feeling that somehow he had known this would happen, that he knew from the first time he saw my wife that this would be the outcome. I suddenly wanted to hate him for his arrogance, his utter conceit. I hated myself for wanting this, but I *did* want it.

"This is…" I whispered, and then paused. I could feel Trinh watching me, waiting for what I was going to say. "I can't believe this is happening."

"Are you complaining?" she said, just loud enough for only me to hear.

"No," I said. My cock was so hard it hurt, straining painfully against my pants, and I shifted anxiously in my seat, desperate to free it.

"Why don't you just take it out?" Trinh said, well aware. "Go ahead. That's what you're here for, right?" Hastily I unfastened my pants and wrenched my aching cock out into the open, immediately wrapping my fist around it and beating it furiously as I listened to my wife's muffled moans, her mouth full with Trey's cock. How many nights had I lain awake, planning this, imagining this? Picturing every possible scenario, every situation; loving every imaginary moment. And now the moment I never imagined would happen had arrived. Here. *Now.* Enraptured, I stared, my fantasy being made reality before my very eyes, and any jealousy I had felt, any uncertainty evaporated, leaving only a consuming urge to see her do this, to see this happen.

The lights from the city had long since faded behind us, and the highway was deserted except for an occasional tractor-trailer. Trinh pushed Raquel past one-ten. The semis blew by, heading into the city, the wind from them buffeting us, crashing against us like thunder, their headlights flashing through the interior of the car for an instant like lighting. I turned around in my seat, abandoning the mirror, all pretense gone now, and watched between the bucket seats as Elisa held Trey's cock up with both hands to look at it. It was huge, every bit as large as Trinh had promised it would be, standing perfectly erect, jutting from his groin, straining up toward Elisa, and Trey brushed my wife's hair from her face to make sure I got a good look.

Elisa gazed up at him as she lapped at his shaft, the weight of Trey's cock resting across her upturned face. Then, hungrily, she hauled it into her empty mouth, sinking down on it until her wet lips were sealed around its base. I could hear her grunting, almost barking as she plunged her mouth over his cock again and again, one hand cupping his fat pouch of balls, the other clamped around the thick base. I watched Trey's cock as I stroked my own, his thick, hard shaft sliding in and out of my wife's wet lips, and I watched Elisa, showing him with her concupiscent gazes and breathless moans how much she loved it. Trey was watching as well, and he was telling Elisa how good she was, how sexy she was, but at that point I don't think Elisa cared whether he thought she was sexy or not.

Trey moved his hands to the back of her head, easing her up or down, whatever felt best to him. Over and over again Elisa worked her mouth around Trey's cock, up and down, back and forth, until she realized that Trey was driving at his own rhythm, and all she need do was hold her head still as his cock pumped through her wet lips. Trey held Elisa's head firmly in his hands and pushed his cock in and out of her mouth like a piston, Elisa's lips stretching around the raised ridges of his shaft.

"Suck it," Trey demanded. "Suck that cock, you little whore." His taunts only seemed to encourage Elisa, his words barely audible over her moans. Trey moved faster, and Elisa slipped a hand under her dress and began to touch herself as

Trey told her again and again how good she was at sucking cock. Her awareness of his pleasure only seemed to intensify her own excitement, and she groaned loudly as he slid his cock into her mouth again and again, almost gagging her every time. I could see her throat contracting, her eyes watering each time he pushed the entire length of his cock into her mouth, and I was certain, given the length of shaft that disappeared between her lips, that his cock was in her throat.

I could feel Trinh staring at me from the driver's seat, gauging my reaction to what was happening. Trey was groaning, his voice desperate as he began to beg Elisa to slow down. I could easily hear Elisa's breathing, heavy and labored as Trey's urgings became more insistent, his moans louder and in rhythm with Elisa's. Suddenly Trey gasped, his fingers tangling into Elisa's hair, his face clenched in anticipation. I saw his chest heave several times as he humped up against Elisa's mouth until finally his body started to convulse. A burst of grunts escaped him, and I knew he was coming in my wife's mouth. He growled out a string of expletives, calling my wife his "little cocksucker," his "filthy whore," and below him Elisa had sealed her lips tightly around his cock, sucking and swallowing until she almost burst from lack of breath.

Their noises promptly lapsed into silence, with the exception of Trey's ragged panting, and Trinh looked at me, smiling. My eyes locked suddenly with Trey's, and for a moment I looked into them. For what, I didn't know. Gratitude, maybe, as absurd as that sounded. But instead, I saw only pride. He seemed to feel conquering, victorious even, and I knew that in his mind he had just taken my wife in a way I never could; that it was Elisa, not him, who had just been pleasured, that he had been gracious enough to allow her to suck his cock; that she had been rewarded with his orgasm.

Elisa looked up at Trey like a child wanting praise, and I watched as she opened her mouth and showed him the shimmering pool of semen on her cupped tongue before she swallowed it.

"You're a lucky man," Trey told me for the second time that night, but this time Elisa seemed to flush with pride at Trey's words. She sat up, tucking her hair behind her ears, and in the headlights of an oncoming vehicle I could see a smile pursing her raw and swollen lips.

I watched the needle sweep past one-forty.

Takes All Comers

AINSLEIGH FOSTER

With the headset on, Ariel looked like an extra from a bad science-fiction movie—or she would have, if she hadn't been wearing her favorite negligee. Let's be honest: *my* favorite negligee. What Ariel likes much of the time, when it comes right down to it, is what turns me on. In that, she's very much a people-pleaser. Which is why it pleased her so to be given slut lessons by her husband while she talked a stranger off.

"You cheat on your husband often?" came the stranger's gruff voice, crackling into his microphone.

Ariel looked at me.

I nodded fervently.

"Oh," she said. "All the time." I made a "keep going" gesture. "Constantly," she said. "With all sorts of guys. Sometimes two, three times a day."

The guy sounded shocked. "Three times a day!?"

I made a so-so gesture.

Ariel got the picture. She started improvising. "Well," she said, "that's a *good* day. I mean, you know, I do have to work and stuff!" I made a gesture so vague I wasn't even sure myself what it meant. Ariel picked up on it and said, "But…you know, between blow jobs to my boss, the other guys I work with, sometimes I'll go out to lunch—"

"Out to lunch!?" the guy choked.

I waved my hands.

"Um…yes?" said Ariel, cocking her head at me.

"With your boss?" asked the guy.

I nodded, waving my hands to indicate that she should nod along with me.

It took her several seconds to remember to say, "Uh-huh?"

There was a long pause, during which I was sure he'd figured it out.

Then he said: "That's so hot."

I grinned and made a thumbs-up.

Ariel winked at me.

"Yeah," she said. "My boss totally takes me out to lunch. Sometimes I even jerk him off under the table. Right there in the restaurant."

The guy was grunting, obviously stroking his cock. I had never fucked guys; I didn't really know what they sounded like when blowing their loads—and especially not the buildup to it—but I was getting used to it.

"Right there in the restaurant?" the guy grunted.

"Right there in the restaurant," said Ariel, her voice thick with sex. Another thumbs-up from me.

"With people watching?" the guy panted.

Ariel delivered her *next* response with the rapture of a student on her first solo flight: "With *everybody* watching. They try not to look, but they know what I'm doing under there." She grew visibly more excited by her sudden surge of erotic creativity. "And if my boss tells me to?"

The guy groaned, hanging on Ariel's every word.

"What? What?" he asked desperately.

"I'll go down under the table and suck him with everyone watching. Just 'cause he likes it."

The guy uttered a bestial strangling sound.

"And 'cause it makes me wet."

"It makes you wet!?" The guy sounded genuinely shocked.

"Uh-huh," said Ariel.

Her hand strayed down between her legs, and she gently caressed her cunt through the soft thin crotch of her teddy.

"Tell me more. Tell me more. What are you wearing?"

Ariel looked confused.

"Wearing now, or when I do this?"

The guy panicked. "I don't know! I don't care!"

She might have been the only phone-sex operator in the history of the business who had actually gone to work in a slinky black teddy with a built-in push-up bra, snap crotch, and black garters leading down to black fishnet stockings with little red bows on them, her perfect feet encased in six-inch black patent-leather heels. She had only herself to blame for this elaborate phone-sex getup. She had told me she'd wear anything I wanted, even instructed me to make her wear the sexiest thing I could imagine her in, because she was doing it all for me.

And she *was* doing it all for me. She didn't need the $2.49 a minute any more than I needed to advertise her online as "Cheating Slutwife Who Takes All Cummers!!!" with blurred-face lingerie shots marked CERTIFIED REAL. She didn't need dirty-minded men from across the nation calling and pouring cumshots in her ear any more than I needed her in a slutty teddy, fishnets, and high heels to be crazy in lust with her.

But none of it hurt our sex life. She was on her sixth call that night, her second night. She decided not to stick to our initial one-night-a-week plan, "just to spice things up." She actually suggested that she could, you know, learn faster if she did it every night for a while. The fact that we'd had fucking incredible hours-long sex last night starting the moment she rang off her shift—that couldn't have had anything to do with it.

Just twenty-four hours ago, Ariel could barely utter the word "fuck" without some hesitation. Now, with only a little prodding from me, she had a mouth like a sailor.

Was I invading the men's privacy? Well…in a word, *yes*. I was listening to them fuck my wife. She was selling a fantasy, and on some level I was invading that fantasy. I was also probably breaking some kind of telecommunications law.

But *fuck*, my dick was hard. Crime had never turned me on so fucking much.

Of course, my favorite teddy was a little worse for wear—last night, she'd worked three hours. But then, I liked her dirty. When she asked to do it again tonight, how could I have told her to wear anything but my favorite?

And besides, describing what she was wearing was a hell of a lot easier when she told the truth.

Though she did pretty well with her business suit, too.

"And when I suck my boss off under the table? I'm wearing a short, tweed skirt, a low-cut, pearl-colored blouse, nude-colored stockings and—"

"Does your husband go down on you?"

Ariel cocked her head at me.

I shrugged.

"When I'm sucking my boss?"

"No," said the guy. "Whenever. Like, tonight. When you go to bed after fucking your boss, will he go down on you?"

I was there before she answered. She gave off a merry little giggle as I buried my face in her crotch.

She tried to shove me away.

I wasn't having it. I kept at her. She kept trying to shove me away, but her heart wasn't in it.

"After I fuck?"

"After you fuck your boss."

"When I'm dirty," she said.

Simon made a hungry, desperate sound.

"Yeah, yeah. Dirty," he said. "Filthy, dirty."

"Dirty."

"Dirty."

"Filthy."

"Filthy."

"Dirty."

"Dirty."

They kept at it like that for a while, saying "Filthy" and "Dirty" back at each other, while Ariel tried to dodge my face and shove me away from her crotch. She even tried to close her thighs, but that was not in the cards—not least because Ariel clearly didn't want it. She just kept saying "Dirty" and

"Filthy" as we both got breathless from our wrestling match. Ariel took greater pleasure in each word with each recitation, Simon clearly becoming more aroused.

"Does he?" he finally asked.

"Well, you know, he does go down on me," she said. "Though not *nearly* as much as he should. No husband ever goes down on his wife as much as he should."

"Don't I know it!" chortled Simon.

"But in fact, he's here right now, and I think—"

"He's there with you?" The guy sounded slightly upset.

"He just got home from work."

"Oh, man," said the guy playfully. "He's gonna be mad you're having phone sex."

"Mmmmm—I don't think so," she said. "You want me to tell him?"

"He'll be mad."

She finally relented and let me get my fingers under the snaps of her crotch. I plucked them away.

"I'm having phone sex," she told me.

I looked shocked.

"Is he mad?" the guy asked. I still couldn't tell if he was amused or dismayed. I didn't care.

"And I fucked my boss at lunch," she said, biting her finger seductively as she looked down at me.

"Oh, man," said Simon. "Is he mad?"

"What do you think?" Ariel asked sexily, looking down at me for guidance.

But I was between her legs. My only answer was that I popped her snap crotch, reached under her ass, and pulled her onto me.

I started working my tongue against her clit, licking her eagerly. She gasped. Punctuating my excitement, I wriggled the tip of my tongue against her supposedly well-fucked entrance. I licked deep and slid two fingers into her. She tasted ripe and tangy—delicious. I started licking her clit.

"He's not mad," sighed Ariel.

"I knew it!" gasped Simon. "He's a cum-lapper, isn't he? He loves it when you're dirty."

"Fuck if I know," breathed Ariel. She arched her back and began to rock against me as I licked her clit.

I shoved my fingers firmly into her and worked her G-spot. She moaned and moved her hips in time with my thrusts. My own headset was getting in the way, so I tore it off.

"Fuck if I know," she repeated. "I don't give a damn, as long as he licks me like that." Then, as if remembering she was getting paid $2.49 a minute to do this, she asked, "How about you, Simon. Are you stroking that big, fat, hard cock for me? I *always* insist that guys stroke their dicks when they're around me."

She tapped my forehead and gestured at me, looking annoyed.

Obediently, I took my cock out. It was hard. I started pumping as I licked her.

"Don't come yet, Simon," Ariel panted. "I want to come for you. Will you let me come for you? For real, I mean?" Simon liked that idea. I licked more firmly, thrusting more deeply, lapping at Ariel's clit as I fingered her.

She must have been damned close already. She leaned back in the chair, lifted her hips, and put one hand on the back of my head, holding me in place so I'd be there as she came. It was her way of saying "Don't stop."

But she said that loud enough with a soft cry of orgasm. She came for Simon, and she came for me. Simon groaned so loud I heard Ariel's headphones crackling.

She moaned: "Oh, yeah, baby, come for me, yeah, baby, stroke that big cock."

She finished coming herself, panting heavily, and said, "Was that good, Simon? Did you come hard, Simon? Simon? Simon?"

"He's gone," I told her, coming up from between her legs.

She frowned bitterly.

"Men," she said. "You're all the same."

"Not all of us," I said. "You still want a good-night kiss?"

She leaned forward and planted one on me.

"Nah," she said. "I think I'll do the kissing. C'mere."

Richard's Secret

SASKIA WALKER

"A gimp?" Richard was a sex slave? Could it be possible? I swallowed, breathed deep, and tried to make sense of what Tom had just told me. "But what does it mean…?" I looked up at him, spluttering the words out. "I mean, I know what it means…I just don't know what he means by it, by approaching us."

Tom rested his hand reassuringly on my shoulder. There was a look of deep concern in his eyes, and he was watching me carefully for my reactions. Oh, how I loved this man; when he had said he had something "a bit heavy" to talk to me about, I thought the worst was about to happen, that he was going to say there was another woman, that he was leaving me. The last thing I expected was for him to reveal this, Richard's secret. Richard's darkest secret.

I had actually known Richard longer than I had Tom. He had been working in the international trade department when

I was transferred to the London branch, about six years earlier. Admittedly he was the dark horse in the department, and the office gossips plagued him with questions about his private life, all of which he managed to avoid and dismiss without being in the least bit offensive.

To me Richard was just a shy, reclusive guy; a small man, and very attractive in an understated way—nicely packaged, dark hair, and vivid blue eyes. I just assumed he was comfortable around me because I was the only one who didn't quiz him about his private life. That was also how I had learned more about him than the tenacious office gossips. He lived alone in an apartment overlooking the Thames and enjoyed a number of extreme sports, like acute and prolonged bouts of mountain biking, martial arts, and kick boxing. I supposed that was what gave him his good packaging—the guy worked out, you know—but none of that seemed to go with his shy, understated image. Neither did this fetishistic sexuality that I had just learned about, but then…maybe it did kind of make sense?

I had kept the personal information he gave me to myself, which is why he liked me, I assumed; he appreciated that kind of respect. Now that I reflected on it, I guessed he had been even friendlier to me since Tom had arrived on the work scene and moved in with me two years ago; but shy single men often feel more comfortable around women who are attached. Little did I know he was observing Tom and me with this kind of proposal in mind. He wanted to be our sex slave, our gimp. My heart rate went up several notches and my body was hot, almost uncomfortably hot. I fanned myself with a magazine while trying to come to terms with the conundrum and the rather extreme affect it was having on me—I had to admit it, the idea made me horny as hell.

"Suzie, I can see you are interested, my love." Tom folded his arms. He was standing in front of me and nodded down at my breasts, where my nipples were swollen and crushed beneath the surface of my silk blouse. There was no hiding it. My sex was clenching, my body was on fire.

"Yes, I can't deny it…the idea of it makes me hot, but you know…I want *us* to be okay." I eyed his long, lean body, the fall of his dark blond hair on his neck. I couldn't bear to lose this man…hell, I could hardly get through a day without wanting us to meld our bodies together and fuck each other senseless.

"It won't affect anything between us, it's just an adventure." He began to stroke my face, pushing back my hair where it was sticking to the damp heat of my neck. "He said he will be transferring soon, so there wouldn't be any awkwardness at work; it would just be a one-off." My, he had thought of everything, and he'd obviously been planning the whole thing for quite a while, too. Tom lifted my chin with one finger, his thumb stroking gently over my lower lip. "He said it would be up to us; he said we could do what we wanted with him." There was a dark, suggestive look in Tom's eyes.

"I see…" I mumbled, not sure if I did.

"One thing I'd like to see…" His voice was hoarse. He ran a finger down the collar of my blouse and into my cleavage. He slipped one finger inside, pulling the blouse open, looking at the shadow between my breasts. His other hand lifted mine and led it to his groin, where his cock was already hard inside his jeans.

"What…?" I wanted to know. The blood was rushing in

my ears; the magazine in my hand fell to the floor.

"I'd like to watch him going down on you." His eyes were filled with lust. I groaned, my hips beginning to shift as I rocked back and forth on the hard kitchen stool, my sex hungry for action. He leaned forward and kissed me, his tongue plunging into my mouth. My fingers fumbled with his fly buttons, and then I was bringing his heavy cock out and stroking it with my whole hand. He pushed me back, over the breakfast bar. He was going to fuck me, right there and then, and I was ready; sweet Jesus was I ready. I hoisted my skirt up around my hips. He dragged my knickers off and pushed my thighs apart with rough, demanding movements. He stroked my inflamed clit, growling when he saw the juices dribbling from my blushing slit. Then he fucked me while I perched on the kitchen stool, pivoting on its hard surface with everything on display.

"Get your tits out," he whispered as he thrust his cock deep inside me, his body crouched over me. I pulled my blouse open, my hands shaking as they shoved my breasts together, kneading them and tweaking the nipples, sending vibrant shivers through my core. I was whimpering, jamming myself down on his thrusting cock as hard as I could. Tom watched with hungry eyes as my hands crushed my breasts. I suddenly remembered Richard blushing when I had caught him looking at me over his monitor, just the other day. Was he aroused then? Had his cock gotten hard as he thought about me and Tom? He had glanced away, furtively, his color high. Dear God, the man had been thinking about us doing this; maybe even thinking about doing this *with* us. He had told Tom his dark secret, and Tom was now rutting in me like a wild man. I was on fire. I whimpered, my hands suddenly clutching at Tom's shoulders. I was about to come. I had never come so bloody fast in my entire life.

"You look very beautiful, Suzie," Richard said. My fingers fidgeted with my neckline nervously. "I always thought you looked like Audrey Hepburn with your hair up like that." He smiled; he seemed quite calm now, and he was leading the situation even though he was going to be the slave. We were nervous, but then we were the novices; presumably he had done this many times before. I glanced at Tom. He had chatted happily about work while we made our way through several glasses of wine, until now—until Richard had moved the conversation on to a personal note. Now Tom had grown silent and watchful.

"Thank you," I replied, swigging another mouthful of wine. Both men were staring at me; the sexual tension had risen dramatically. "It's the little black dress," I added, with a smile. That morning I had told myself that I wasn't dressed any differently; I always wore stockings, garters, and high heels to the office. The little black dress underneath my jacket was the new addition. It was very soft and clingy, and now that I had abandoned the jacket I felt good in it. Besides, what does one wear when one is about to take on a sex slave?

"You want to know what I've got in the briefcase, don't you?" He'd seen me looking at his black leather briefcase when we left the office that evening, the three of us headed to Tom's and my place for drinks. Yes, I had been curious. I nodded. "I like to wear a mask," he said. "I've brought it with me, and I'd like you to put it on for me."

My sex twitched. The combination of power and deviance

he had suggested in that simple comment hit my libido like a narcotic entering the bloodstream.

"Okay, I'll do it," I replied, as nonchalantly as I could manage.

Richard stood up, taking off his immaculate suit jacket as he did so, and placing it over the arm of the sofa. He picked up the briefcase and carried it over to the breakfast bar, where he set it down, flicked the combination lock, and opened it. Tom and I both watched with bated breath. Richard undid his tie, rolling it slowly and tucking it into a section in the top of the briefcase. Then he lifted something out of the case and turned back to us, leaving the briefcase sitting open on the breakfast bar. As he walked back to me, I stood up.

"It's perfectly safe," he said, allaying any concerns we might have in advance. "It was handmade, for me." He passed the soft, black leather mask into my hand. I turned it, feeling it with my fingers. It was cool to the touch and incredibly soft, molded, with laces down the back and breathing holes for the nose, a closed zip over the mouth. A powerful jolt went through me when I realized that there were no eye holes; Richard would not be able to see what we were doing once he had the mask on. My eyes flitted quickly to Tom, and I saw that he had noticed that too. Richard undid his shirt, revealing well-muscled shoulders and torso. He dropped it on the sofa and stood in his black pants, looking from one to the other of us, for our consent.

"Turn around, and I'll put it on." Even as I heard my own voice another wave of empowerment roared over me. Richard smiled slightly and inclined his head.

Tom suddenly stood up. "I think you should take that

dress off, first," he instructed. The mask dangled from my hand. Richards's eyelids fell as he looked at the floor, hanging his head, but I could see that he was smiling to himself. The atmosphere positively hummed with sexual tension. Tom's instruction had completed the dynamics of the triangle. This was it; the scene was set for action.

I put the mask down on the coffee table and pulled the soft jersey dress up and over my head.

"You can take one look at her, before she puts your mask on." Tom's eyes glittered. Richard's head moved as he looked back over to my stiletto-heeled shoes, up to my stockings and the scrap of fine French lace barely covering my crotch, then up and on to the matching balconette bra that confined my breasts. I knew I looked statuesque and glamorous in this, my most expensive underwear, and I could see that he approved.

"Thank you," he said, his gaze sinking to the floor again. Before he turned his back he passed something else into Tom's hands. It was a set of intricately carved manacles. As Tom looked down at the object, Richard turned his back, bent his head, and put his wrists behind his back—awaiting both the mask and the manacles. Not only would he not be able to see, he wouldn't be able to touch. Tom looked at me, his eyebrows lifting, a wicked smile teasing the corners of his mouth.

Tom came forward and enclosed Richard's strong wrists in the manacles. Then it was my turn to take action and I moved over, heart pounding, and began to ease the mask over his head. It pulled easily into place and I gently tightened the laces, gauging my way until the mask was molded tight and secure over his face. When the knot was done Richard slowly descended to the floor and squatted down on his knees, eyes unseeing, his head cocked, as if awaiting instructions.

We circled him, taking in the look of this creature, as he had now become, kneeling between us in the center of our personal space. I had prepared the room well, with the furniture pushed back and subdued lighting. He knelt between us with his masked head lifted up and back, his strong arms manacled behind him, his cock a discernible hard outline in his pants. With Tom towering over him, Richard presented an image I would never forget.

Tom nodded at me, pushed an armchair forward, and indicated that I sit down.

"Do you remember what I said?" He kissed me, then pulled my knickers down the length of my legs and up, over my heels, stroking my ankles as he did so. I nodded. "Good." He smiled—it was devastating, wicked—and then he grabbed our slave around the back of the neck and urged him forward. "Your mistress is one horny bitch. I want you to go down on her, and make sure you do the job properly. I'll be watching." With that, he unzipped the mouth on the mask and slowly lowered Richard's head into the heat between my thighs.

I couldn't believe this was happening—Tom was so dominant, so strong and commanding. I was getting wetter by the second. I couldn't look down at the man between my thighs; I felt a sudden rush of embarrassment and strangeness as he crouched there, unseeing and yet so sexual. My eyes followed Tom as he moved away. He was looking into the briefcase that had been left open on the breakfast bar. What was in the briefcase? I wondered, again. Then I felt the surface of the mask, cold against my thighs as Richard moved his head along them, feeling his way toward the hot niche at their juncture.

The tip of his tongue stuck out, and I felt its blissful touch in the sticky, cloying heat of my slit. He used his tongue like a digit, exploring the territory of my sex, before he began mouthing me, his tongue lapping against my swollen lips and over the jutting flesh of my clit. It felt so good; my embarrassment was quickly replaced by something else: sheer rampant lust. I tried to stay calm and take my time; I had to resist the urge to gyrate on the edge of the seat and push myself into his obedient face.

After a moment I became aware of Tom's presence again and looked up, gasping for breath. He had stripped off his shirt, his leanly muscled chest bared for my eager eyes. I purred; he blew me a kiss, and then grinned.

"Stop now." At the sound of the order Richard's head lifted, cocking to one side again. "I've found some of your other toys and I intend to use them. Do you understand?" Richard nodded. My fingers clutched at my clit, replacing the tongue, keeping myself on the edge while I tried to see what Tom was holding in his hands.

He pocketed a shiny blue condom packet and gestured at Richard with a stiff leather cock harness. Tom looked dangerous now. He always had a certain edginess about him during sex, but I'd never seen him quite this intense before.

"You really are a deviant one, aren't you?" He gave a deep chuckle. Richard hung his head in shame. "Oh, but there's no need to be so embarrassed; we can both see you've got a stiffy, Richard." With that he crouched down on the floor and grabbed at Richard's belt. He opened the buckle, the button, and zipper in the blink of eye and, yes, Richard did have a stiffy—a major stiffy.

"You are a bad boy, and did you get hard when you had

a taste of Suzie?" Richard nodded. "Right, I'm going to have to take care of this. No one said you were allowed to get a hard-on, did they?" He pulled Richard forward so he was kneeling straight up, his pants falling down around his knees. He wasn't wearing underwear and my eyes roved over him in appreciation. Tom pushed Richard's head to one side and bent down, his hand measuring the other man's cock in a hard vigorous fist. God, what a sight! I shot two fingers inside my slit, probing myself while I watched Tom handle Richard's cock.

With some effort, he pushed the cock harness over Richard's erection and secured it with the stud fastener around his balls. He was almost entirely covered. I could just see his balls squeezed up inside the circles of leather and the very head of his cock pushing out of its containment. The harness was extremely tight, and I could see the effect it was having on Richard, his whole body growing more rigid by the second, as if he was being gripped in a hard heavy hand, his blood-filled cock bursting for release.

"Get back to work on Suzie, right now." Tom pushed him back between my thighs. By then I was on the very edge of the chair, my legs spread wide to get more of him. Tom walked behind him and pulled the condom out of his pocket, turning it over in his hands. He looked at me; his green eyes glittered like gemstones. His eyebrows lifted imperceptibly and his mouth was fixed in a devilish smile. He wanted my approval. I whimpered, my head barely nodding, but I really wanted to see him doing it. Tom opened his fly and got out his rock-hard cock. He pumped it in his hands for a moment, his eyes on mine. This was one of my favorite sights; I couldn't get enough of seeing him with his hands on his cock, and he knew it. He looked down at my chest, growling. I followed his gaze and saw that my nut-hard nipples were jutting up from the edges of my bra, my breasts oozing out of the restraining fabric.

Tom eased the condom on and then knelt down behind Richard. When Richard felt his legs being pushed apart his mouth stopped moving and clamped over my sex. His body was rigid between us, his buttocks on display to Tom, his face pushing in against my sex, his muscled arms bound tightly behind his back. If I rolled my head to one side I could see his harnessed cock.

He remained quite still, his tongue in my hole, when Tom began to probe him from behind. Tom's face contorted and I felt Richard's head thrust in against me as he was entered from behind. My hips were moving fast on the chair, moving my desperate sex flesh up and down against the leather mask, his mouth, and the rough edges of the zipper. I couldn't help it, I was gone on this.

Richard's cock looked fit to burst. Tom pulled out and ploughed in deeper, his teeth bared with effort and restraint. He must have hit the spot, because Richard's body tensed and arched, his tongue going soft and limp against my clit. I glanced down and saw his cock riding high and tight in its harness, then it spurted up under his arched body, which was convulsing.

"You made him come," I cried accusingly, but with delight, and a dark laugh choked in my throat. Tom grinned at me and then jammed into him hard again.

"Suck her good, Richard; I want Suzie to come next."

Our obedient slave began to tongue me again. I gasped my pleasure aloud for Tom—Tom, my gorgeous lover, watching me. It was just like our sessions of mutual masturbation, but with Richard's darkest secret filling the void between us; tonight he was the gap across which we watched each other's deepest pleasures rising up and taking us over.

Tom's lean body was taut, his hands gripping on to Richard's hips, the sinuous muscles in his arms turning to rope. His eyes were locked on mine, urging me on as he sent Richard's tongue lashing my clit again and again with each deep thrust. I began to buck, wildly out of control, shock waves going right through the core of my body and under the skin of my scalp as wave after wave of relief flooded over me, and then Tom threw back his head, roaring his release as his hips jerked repeatedly and he shot his load.

Tom sat across the breakfast bar from me. He sipped the rich black Colombian coffee I had made us, his fingertips running against mine as he eyed me over his cup. He smiled as he put the cup down and lifted my fingers to his lips.

"You looked incredible," he whispered, kissing my fingertips. It was an extremely intimate moment; he was looking at me with possessiveness and something akin to awe.

"So did you," I replied and I meant it; I was overwhelmed by my lover. Richard had long since left us, but the images he had given us of each other would be with us for a very long time.

"Do you think we'll ever see him again?"

"Maybe," he replied. "Maybe not. Would it bother you if we did?"

I gave it some thought. I pictured us casually speaking to him in the office, the way we used to, but this time the three of us would be looking at each other and knowing what had gone on. The idea of it made my pulse quicken again.

"No, not in the least." I liked the idea. I smiled at Tom. Not only had we seen each other anew, but Tom and I had become part of Richard's secret, part of Richard's darkest secret.

Performance Art
OSCAR WILLIAMS

You're so proud of them, and I don't blame you. They're lovely, large on your frame but perfectly proportioned. Double-Ds, and all natural, you brag in the online profile you use to scout for potential partners. You're only five-three, perhaps 110 pounds, so I suspect no one believes you—but I know you're telling the truth, and calling them double-Ds is, in a way, being conservative. They strain against your bras, stretching the cups, showing curvaceous and enticing through the tight sweaters you wear. You love that men look at them. It's like you can feel their energy, radiating from their eyes, caressing your tits, unbuttoning your top, unhitching your bra, untying your bikini top, lifting your sweater over your head, revealing them. It's as if you can feel a man's gaze undressing you, devouring your tits. When you know a man is checking them out it's like he's stroking your nipples with his eyes, whether we're sitting in a restaurant, lounging on the beach, dancing at a club, or just walking down the street. And you invite it. You encourage it, because you love the attention. You wear revealing tops and go without a bra when you really shouldn't, relishing the caress of the male gaze over the curves of your full breasts. Women, too; nothing makes you hotter than thinking that another woman, straight, bi, or gay, has just checked out your tits.

You're all about showing off. You're a total exhibitionist, and you've got the body to indulge yourself. But it's your tits that really drive people crazy, and that's why you love them so much. When you see people whispering, wondering if your tits are fake, I know it turns you on even more. People can't seem to stop obsessing over your incredible tits. No one can believe you were born with the genes to produce such flawless orbs, but you were, and every pair of eyes that caresses them is a chance for you to brag.

And it's not just that they're so big and perfect to look at, that they're so firm that you don't need a bra, that they defy gravity as surely as if they were bought and paid for in a plastic surgeon's office but much, much more attractive of shape. Your whole sexuality seems to revolve around your tits. Your nipples get incredibly hard when you're turned on. Those pink circles are so sensitive that I sometimes make you come just by pinching them, growling at you to spread your legs wider so you can't rub your thighs together. Sometimes it takes hours. Sometimes you don't come at all, but just having your nipples played with drives you crazy. If you aren't able to come just from having them rubbed and pinched, not being allowed to touch your clit, then invariably by the time I tire of our little game you're tottering right on the edge. The first stroke of my cock into your sopping-wet pussy brings you off, making you moan and buck and thrust with orgasm.

Other times, you drop to your knees and take my cock in your mouth, sucking hungrily as you play with your own tits—and then eagerly sliding them around my shaft. You push them together and let me tit-fuck you, relinquishing your grip on them and letting me do the holding only when you're soaring close to orgasm—so you can reach down and rub your clit the few strokes it takes to get you off. When I come on your tits, you go mad, coming harder, rubbing my thick jizz into your luscious globes. Licking your fingers.

I've always loved that you're such a tit whore. I've always adored the fact that you want to show them off, that you want your tits to be looked at. I bought you a novelty shirt once that said, *Look at my chest when you're talking to me,* as a joke. You didn't hesitate; you wore it everywhere for a few weeks, usually without a bra. You meant it, too, and guys who talked to you didn't know what to think. Most of them would nervously fix their eyes to yours, but I would see them glancing down, the same way they always did but this time wracked with guilt, knowing you could tell. It would make you flirt harder than ever. It would make your nipples get hard, braless in the tight T-shirt, showing through sweat-dampened cotton. It would make your pussy wet, and whenever you wore that shirt you would tear off my clothes the second we got home, would come like a waterfall the second my cockhead entered your pussy.

When we went to a topless beach with some friends, you were the first of the women to doff your top, and I could see your nipples stiffening as they moistened, sweaty in the sun. The men on the ridge with their video cameras all trained their long-distance lenses on you, and I could see the effect it was having on you. As I rubbed suntan lotion into your tits, I could feel you squirming against me, and I knew if I'd managed to slip my finger into your pussy without being seen, you would have been incredibly wet. You were indulging in your favorite brand of performance art: the big tease, to anyone who would watch. By the time I got you back to the car to drive to the burger place for a beachside lunch, you couldn't wait any longer. You sucked me off in the car, bent over with your face in my lap and your blonde hair bobbing rhythmically up and down—not caring who was watching. I pinched your nipples as you sucked me, and I let you rub your thighs together this time. You came before I did, your face pressed to my spit-slick cock, your breasts clutched tight in my hands, your nipples pulsing with each hard pinch I gave them. You finished me off with your mouth, hungry for my come.

We go to play parties occasionally—parties where S/M aficionados go to show off. You always wear something revealing over your tits—a patent-leather bra, a see-through lace top, a mesh T-shirt. You get wetter, your nipples harder, with every man that looks guiltily at them, lusting, every woman who enviously compliments your "outfit," knowing what they're really thinking: "My God, look at those tits."

When we go down into the dungeon and start to play, I always know what you want. To have your top half stripped and your tits played with until you're driven crazy. Letting everyone see just how magnificent they are in their full, naked glory. Another kind of performance art, once again focused on your favorite two things in the world: your tits.

In fact, performance art is what gave me the idea for our

little scene. I once read an article about a performance artist whose form of art was to put a box around her upper body and walk around the street, encouraging passersby to put their hands through the holes cut in the front of the box and feel her tits. I know you would love to do that, letting anyone who wanted to stroke their fingers around your perfect mounds, pinching the nipples, making you come. Except that you'd never do it, because it wouldn't be the same for you if people couldn't see them.

But it's still a compelling idea. And that's where I got the brainstorm. How to finally satisfy that need you have to let every man in the world—or at least every man in the room—fuck your tits.

I take you to the play party late, so it's already going strong and crowded by the time we get there. In the dressing room, I strip you down to your new outfit—peekaboo corset that comes up just under your breasts, leaving them bare, covering only your belly, back, and crotch. It's nothing more than a string between your asscheeks. Wrist restraints aren't enough for tonight; I put on a posture collar to keep your head up straight, and slide your arms into a bondage sleeve, cinching it tight so your arms are thrust behind you, forcing you to keep your back up straight too—and present your bare breasts to anyone who cares to look.

Or touch.

With a leash attached to your posture collar, I lead you into the main lounge area. I see a trio of men dressed in leather eyeing your tits admiringly. I lead you over and nudge you in the back.

"Would you like to touch them, Sir?" you ask, as I've instructed you to do.

"What?"

"M…my tits," you stammer. "You can touch them if you like."

The three men look at me for permission, and I nod. One of them reaches out and begins to caress your tits. You moan softly. I nudge you again in the back.

"Your mouth, too," you say, your voice hoarse. "You can use your mouth on them."

The man bends low, his bearded mouth closing around your firm, erect nipple. He begins to suckle you as his friend takes the other breast, licking and sucking it as you whimper gently and squirm against me. I hold you up and force you into their grasp. One of them is finished with you; his friend takes his place, suckling your nipple and biting it roughly. I don't move to stop him, even though I can tell it's too intense for you. After all, you've got your safeword.

I slide my hand around your body, draw my fingers up your thighs, and wedge them between your legs, under the crotch of your corset. You're very, very wet.

You've attracted a small crowd. I sit you on a stool nearby and hold you there while you invite other men to come suckle your nipples. Women, too; you've never been with a woman, but tonight your breasts belong to all takers.

"Say it," I whisper into your ear.

You look at me desperately, hungrily, knowing you must obey.

"I'll be in the dungeon in a few minutes," you say, your voice raspy from the pleasure flowing through your tits as strangers suckle your nipples. "Any of you men who want to can visit me and come on my tits."

An approving murmur goes around the room. I check you again and find you're even wetter than before. After a few dozen more strangers suckle your breasts for a few minutes at a time, I decide you've had enough. I lead you out of the lounge area and down to the dungeon.

I choose a central location, laying you out on a low platform at just the right height. I undo your bondage sleeve and stretch your arms over your head, buckling on the restraints and padlocking them to the top of the table. I do the same to your ankles, keeping your legs together.

A group of men has followed us down into the dungeon, waiting for their opportunity to come on your tits. Several of them already have their hard cocks out and are stroking them.

"Just the tits," I tell them, stepping back. "You can only come on her tits."

"With pleasure," one says, and leans over you, looking into your frightened eyes as he strokes his cock, aiming it at your full, firm mounds. When he shoots his load over your breasts, you whimper softly, the humiliation mingled with excitement. He rubs his cockhead over your breasts, smearing the cream into your nipples and cleavage.

Another one takes his place, climbing onto the table and straddling you as he pumps his cock over your tits.

I watch as three, then four, then ten, then twenty men crouch over you and come on your tits. You're covered soon, your breasts slick with jism. You're moaning, and when I come around to the end of the table and slip my hand up into your crotch, you almost come at that moment.

As men continue to use you, jerking off all over your tits, I unclasp your ankles, spread them apart, and clip them to the corners of the table, spreading your legs. I can see your fear: Am I now going to let the men fuck you?

But you've exhausted all the men in the party. Female submissives shoot you angry glares, their masters' orgasms having been co-opted for your degradation. Your tits are covered with cream, glistening with it, your corset soaked. A pool of it has formed under your shoulders. I unsnap your crotch and pull the leather-lined spandex up, revealing your pussy. I take out my own cock and, climbing onto the table, slip it between your swollen pussy lips. I enter you with a hard thrust, and your eyes go wide as you lift your hips to meet me. I start to fuck you, giving you your much-deserved reward, and a cheer goes up from the men who just shot on your tits. I come down on top of you and my chest rubs against their semen, reminding you of how you've been used. I pound into you and it's not long before you come, thrusting under me, begging me to fuck you harder. Your moans of orgasm bring another cheer from the men, approving of the way you've been rewarded for giving them your all.

When you're finished coming, I pull out, crouch over you, and unload my cock on your breasts. Streams hit your face and I rub them in too, feeling you lick my fingers clean as I push them into your mouth.

There's a faint round of applause as I zip up and unclasp your restraints. I quickly wipe down the table and smear the excess semen onto your breasts again. I put your bondage sleeve back on and lead you up the stairs, your breasts dripping come, your face red from shame and post-orgasmic pleasure. When we reach the showers, I soap you up and hose you down, then lead you into the dressing room.

You put your street clothes back on and I lead you into the world, knowing your ordeal will weigh heavily on your mind from now on, dominating your thoughts whenever a man looks at your tits. In the car, you look at me and smile, humiliation giving way to release, giving way to fondness.

I kiss you on the lips, and your tongue grazes mine. I put the car in gear and we drive away.

Dress Me Up

ERICA DUMAS

I love it when you dress me up. Well, you don't dress me up, exactly—though that's how I like to think of it. I put on the clothes, but you pick them out. When we play this way, you come over to my apartment and let yourself in using the key I gave you, never telling me what clothes you'll select for me. And they're always so much more revealing than I would have dared pick out for myself.

Tonight it's my tiniest white minidress, with a matching white lace thong, push-up bra, and garter belt. It's all laid out on the bed, with a handwritten note from you saying *Don't be late*. The stockings are white, too—seamed down the back to accentuate the curve of my legs. The white shoes you picked out for me have six-inch heels: fuck-me shoes. Fuck-me-*hard* shoes. Fuck-me-*till-I-scream* shoes.

And I know you will.

They're all mine, but I would never wear them all

together. The dress I probably wouldn't wear at all—it's much too naughty, too daring. I bought it with you in mind, knowing you would make me wear it. Just the way I want you to.

You set out my jewelry, too—a pearl and gold choker, matching earrings, matching bracelets. These aren't mine; they're new. The kind of gifts you'd give a prostitute. It turns me on to hold them, feel their weight in my hands. I don't worry about how you can afford all this; I know I'm worth it, because I'm your whore. And I know tonight I'll be the best whore in town.

I put it all on slowly after my long, luxurious bath, savoring the way the skimpy clothes reveal my body. I put on my makeup extra-thick, the sexy clothes inspiring me to paint myself like a slut. Then I do my hair the same way—big hair, porn-star hair. A whore's hair.

There's no purse and no watch—tonight I'm at your mercy. I know you'll take care of me.

You ring the buzzer at exactly seven, and I grab my jacket and head for the door. Then I stop and think, and put down my jacket—you didn't lay it out, so I won't wear it. I'm not to wear anything you didn't give me.

I hope it's not too cold tonight.

When you see me, I know you're pleased with the way I've filled out your selections. Your eyes rove over me as I approach the car. My breasts stretch the top of the minidress, and the push-up bra shows them to full advantage. It *is* a little chilly out, and I notice right away that my nipples are hardening under the dress, so much so that they're quite visible. My face reddens, but I don't move to cross my arms. I want you to see. I want everyone to see.

You lean over and kiss me, letting your hand rest on my belly and trail up a little to casually brush my tits. I shudder as you do; it sends a pulse of sensation from my breasts to my pussy. I shift uncomfortably on the seat as your lips curve in a smile; you can tell how turned on I am, and how the nervousness heightens my arousal.

"You look nice," you tell me.

It's all I need to hear. If you gushed over me, told me what a sexy slut I am, it would be too much. All I need is to know that I've satisfied you, that you're happy with the way I look. The fact that you've dressed me up like your tart is just the icing on the cake.

"Where are we having dinner?" I ask.

"Somewhere everyone can look at you," you tell me, and turn the heat on.

Somehow that excites me even more—the silent acknowledgment that you can tell how hard my nipples are, that you know it's not just the cold. My heart pounds as I sink into the luxurious heat blowing from the vents. You pull away from the curb.

People look at me as they pass by in cars or cross the street in front of us when we're stopped at lights. They can't see much, but they can see enough. They know I'm a slutty little bird. That's enough to make my pussy feel hot, to make my clit rub against the too-tight thong you've selected. The thong is entirely made of lace, see-through and a little rough, reminding me how hard my clit is. I know if I checked I'd find myself wet.

You take me downtown. You pull up outside the most expensive hotel in town, and the valets ogle me as they take the car keys.

I'm aware of all the eyes on me as we walk across the lobby. My nipples are still quite hard, with no hope of being any different until you've fucked me hard. You take me to the tower elevator and push the button. Businessmen look at me, trying to glance away so it doesn't look like they're looking. You have your arm around me and you pull me close, staring them down with a little smile on your face.

In the crowded elevator, you push the button for the top floor: CAFE SKYE. I lean close to you, half frightened that I'll feel a hand up my skirt—and half wanting to. The elevator empties out as we travel up ten floors, twenty, stopping every few floors as people disembark. Then I *do* feel a hand up my skirt. Yours—I think. I lean back onto it and feel your finger slipping between my cheeks, plucking the crotch of the thong out of the way. Easing between my barely-parted legs. Touching my wet pussy.

I have to stifle a gasp as your finger creeps forward to touch my swollen clit. It's your hand all right—no one can touch my clit like that. My knees almost buckle; my whole body feels like it's about to melt. You rub me as the elevator empties out, until there's only one man left. Then he leaves, one floor before the restaurant.

When the doors close, you grab me and push me against the wall. I moan as I sink into your grasp. You press your mouth to mine and your tongue invades me, pushing hard against mine. I can feel your cock hard in your pants, pressing against my belly. Even with the six-inch heels, I'm shorter than you. Your left hand cups one breast, your palm rubbing my nipple through the thin fabric, nudging it until it pops out of the bra cup and stretches the white dress, hidden from the world only by the thinnest of gossamer fabrics. Then you reach in and gently ease my breast out of the dress, making it press against the arm strap, tucking my bra cup underneath. Your other hand, now curved more fully under my ass, pushes firmly against my clit and then you ease your fingers back, fucking two of them into me.

I almost come right there.

The elevator dings and you turn away from me, leaving me panting and weak against you. I move my hand to tuck my breast back into my bra, into the dress, but you gently take my wrist and pull it away.

You tuck my breast in instead, always the protector—and always in control.

My face hot with excitement, I put my arms at my sides as we walk into the restaurant.

The maître d' eyes me, scandalized by my slutty dress. He opens his mouth like he's going to say something, but then he decides not to. As he looks through his reservation book to find your name, his eyes keep slipping up to my breasts. My nipples are showing plainly through the dress. Perhaps he thinks I'm unaware of how skimpy the dress is, that I'm not used to dressing in such a revealing fashion.

Perhaps he thinks I'm a dirty whore, showing off to any man who will look.

You hold out a twenty-dollar bill.

"Right in the middle of the restaurant, please," you say. "We're here to see and be seen."

"Evidently," he murmurs, and accepts the bill, tucking it into his tuxedo jacket.

He leads us over to our table in a section in the center

of the room on a raised dais where everyone can see me. As I pass through the room behind you, all the male diners, to a man, look at me. Their wives shoot me dirty looks. Every pair of eyes touching my hard nipples sends a wave of pleasure into my cunt. I know my thong is soaked by now. Dripping. You smile at me, glancing around to make sure everyone is looking. They're trying not to, but they can't help it. My knees feel weak as the maître d' holds out my chair. Perhaps it's an accident that his arm brushes one of my nipples as he hands me the menu. Either way, it sends an explosion of sensation from my nipple to my cunt. I can feel my clit throbbing hard in my soaked thong. It makes me even more aware that men are looking at my tits, looking at me, studying my exposed nipple. Wanting me, but hating me. A whore, showing off for everyone.

I don't notice much about the food or the service or the supposedly spectacular view. What I notice is you looking at me throughout dinner; undressing me with your eyes; taking off my tiny dress and my slutty underwear; using your gaze to tug my other breast out of my bra, out of the dress, to show off both my tits to everyone. I'm so wet I'm afraid I'll soak through the dress, leave a wet chair behind. In fact, I'm pretty sure I will.

But I also notice the patrons whispering, pointing at me. I notice the kitchen help, beautiful brown-skinned boys with wide shoulders, filling water glasses and pointing at me, bending close to mutter comments to each other while looking right at me. One busboy in particular fills my water glass every time I take a sip. He looks at me and smiles, his eyes filled with lust. And I notice our waiter, looking at me salaciously with mingled contempt and desire.

And I notice you leaning forward over the table, feeding me chocolate cake for dessert, a tiny forkful at a time. Each bite makes me wish it was you in my mouth.

After you've paid the bill, you reach across the table and leave a hotel key card in a paper sleeve with a room number on it.

"I'm going to the room," you tell me. "Have a drink at the bar and meet me at the room. But don't come down for at least an hour. I'll be there all night, so take your time."

"You'll…you'll leave our tab open? I…I don't have any money," I say apologetically.

You shake your head. "No," you tell me. "I've already closed it out."

"Then…how can I get a drink?" My voice is quivering, half from arousal, half from fear. I'm terrified of what you have in store for me, but my clit is pulsing with anticipation. This humiliation is agony, but I swear if you don't fuck me soon I'm going to come spontaneously, without ever touching my clit.

You lean forward and smile, pointing with your finger. "See that man at the bar?" you ask me.

I glance over; there's a gray-haired man, perhaps sixty, dressed in an expensive suit. He's sitting alone, sipping whiskey from a highball glass. He's looking at me hungrily, not even caring that you've noticed him.

"Do you see him?" you ask me.

"Yes," I say, my eyes locked on the gray-haired man.

"You're going to get him to buy you a drink," you tell me. "And you're going to pay him back for it. Every time he offers you another drink, you'll accept it and finish it quickly. Within ten minutes. If he buys you one drink, you'll get him alone and give him a hand job. And let him come on your tits."

"Oh, God," I whimper. "You must be joking...."

"Not at all," you say. "I'm dead serious. If he buys you two drinks, you'll suck his cock and let him fuck you. And stroke him off onto your face when he's ready to go. Three drinks..."

You lean closer, smiling, looking into my horrified, humiliated face, knowing the effect your words are having on my aching cunt.

"Three drinks?" I whisper in a small, frightened voice.

"Three drinks, and he gets to fuck you in the ass," you tell me.

I shiver.

"What if he doesn't want to?" I ask.

"Come now," you say. "He's a man. All you have to do is ask him, and I'm sure he'll put his cock in whatever hole you offer."

"How...how?" is all I can say.

"You're a talented girl. You know about the birds and the bees."

"Where am I supposed to take him?"

"Perhaps he has a room," you tell me. "Or perhaps you can do him in the hallway, like any other whore. He looks like he's got money, darling. I hope you brought some lube."

I shake my head. "No, I didn't bring anything."

"Then I hope you're good and turned on by the time he puts it in your ass," you tell me. "I guess you didn't bring a condom either."

I shake my head again. "Nothing. You told me not to bring anything."

You chuckle. "I did, did I? Well, then, no condom. I guess you really should know about the birds and the bees by the time the evening is over. Men always prefer the feel of a naked pussy—or asshole. So I'm sure he'll appreciate it when you let him fuck you bare."

You get up from the table, bend over, and kiss me on the cheek.

"At least an hour, darling," you tell me. "But take your time. If he wants to fuck you all night, I'll be waiting. And as soon as he finishes with you, come to my room ready for more. I'm sure you'll just be getting warmed up."

You leave me there, panting, my face red. The busboys are eyeing me, particularly the one who has just appeared to fill my water glass. His arm brushes my nipple as he bends over, and I don't pull away. I'm too confused, too excited. I can smell his sharp sweat. I look over to the bar and see the man you've picked out for me. Thirty years older than me, if he's a day. He's leering at me openly.

Weakly, I smile at him.

I walk over on trembling legs and sit down next to him. He looks at me hungrily. Not knowing what to do with the key card clutched in my hand—of course I don't have any pockets—I lay it on the bar in front of me, making a mental note that under no circumstances can I let myself forget it.

The bartender appears in front of me, his face twisted in a look of disgust. He must be thinking I'm like any high-class hotel whore, working the restaurant.

"Can I get you something?" he sneers.

"I...I need a moment to decide," I say.

The bartender disappears and the man next to me leans

close. "Hi," he says to me. "Here alone?"

I take a deep breath, barely able to speak. I can feel tears forming in my eyes. A little sob grabs my throat when I try to say something.

I cover up for it quickly, speaking in a tormented voice, plainly edging toward tears.

"I am now," I tell the man. "My boyfriend just broke up with me."

"Oh, baby, I'm sorry," he said. "What's your name?"

"Erica," I tell him.

"Erica, I'm Hal. Let me buy you a drink."

"I shouldn't," I say. "I shouldn't drink after a shock like that."

"Sure you should," Hal tells me, waving the bartender over. "Beautiful girl like you, first thing you need to do is have some fun. Get him back for being a careless bastard. I can't believe he'd let a girl like you go." He gestures at the bartender. "Mike, let's get this girl a whiskey sour. Whiskey sour, Erica?"

"That'd be fine," I say, my eyes glistening with tears of fright. That's one drink. I'm going to give him a hand job.

"And make it extra-strong," says Hal under his breath, leaning close to Mike the bartender, perhaps thinking he's speaking quietly enough that I can't hear. "She's having a rough night." His eyes lock in on my exposed nipple, and he licks his lips.

"One whiskey sour," says the bartender, leering at me contemptuously.

One drink. I'm going to stroke his cock. I'm going to jerk him off. I'm going to pump him until he comes on my tits. My clit throbs painfully against the bar stool.

The drink comes and I gulp it desperately while Hal tries to make small talk. He wants to know more details about the break up.

"He...he wants to see other people," I say. "He...he says I can't...can't satisfy him."

"Oh, now, that's a shame. He must be crazy. Pretty girl like you, I'm sure you have a healthy libido. Want a refill on that?"

I want to say no. I want to refuse the drink, run to you, hide in your arms. But you've ordered me to accept, to take Hal's liquor and let him do what he wants to me. To let him get me drunk and fuck me with increasing intimacy depending on how drunk he gets me. I know I have to say yes. I know I have to let Hal buy me as many drinks as he wants, and for each drink, his cock will invade a new part of my body. This is the second drink. It means I'm going to suck his cock and let him fuck me. And when he's ready to come, I'm going to jerk him off on my face.

My voice quavers as I try to speak. I clear my throat. "Yes," I manage to croak, already feeling the heady effects of the whiskey mingling with the wine from dinner. "I'll have another."

Mike mixes another whiskey sour while Hal tells me he's single. I know he's lying, but I don't care. I know I can't refuse him. The least he's going to get, now, is my mouth, clamped around his cock. My face, presented to him for defilement. His come, shooting all over me. I can already feel hot streams hitting me. The humiliation makes me turn deep red, my body flushing hot. I can feel my cunt pulsing between my tightly closed thighs.

"Drink up, darling."

I try to make it last, but I can't. I'm so nervous every time I take a sip it turns into a gulp. By the time the ice rattles in the glass, I can feel I'm getting drunk. The whiskey is enveloping my head, taking me over. When I'm finished, Hal doesn't even ask. He just waves Mike over and orders another for me.

Three drinks. He can do whatever he wants to me—fuck my mouth, my pussy, my ass.

"Thank you," I say. "I feel like I'm taking advantage of you, letting you buy me all these drinks."

Hal chuckles. "Oh, I can afford it," he says. "And from the looks of it, you can too." His eyes rivet to my exposed nipple as he says it.

The whiskey sour goes quickly while Hal describes what a romantic he is. The right way to treat a woman. Make her feel special. I can smell the scent of Hal's body, the aroma of his sweat. I glance down at his crotch and see that his cock is halfway hard. He's leaning closer to me as he talks. His hand is on my thigh, up above the top of my stockings, past where the garters clip to the gossamer fabric. His fingers creep up under the hem of my dress. My flesh tingles as he touches me. I let my legs slip slightly open, and his fingers creep up still further—a planned invasion disguised as a casual, friendly gesture.

I'm going to spread my legs and feel his cock, naked, raw, latex-free, sliding into my pussy. I'm going to feel him hump into me, fuck me until he comes inside me. I'm going to go back down to your hotel room with Hal's come leaking out of my cunt. I find myself leaning against Hal, my hand grazing his thigh. When I shift slightly, I feel the press of his cock, half-hard against my palm. One hand creeps further up my dress, stroking my thighs. His other hand is on my arm, gripping me, steadying me from my drunken sway on the bar stool—or making sure I can't get away.

He thinks I don't see. He thinks I don't see him as he takes his hand from my thigh, reaches into his jacket pocket, turns away with a pill bottle in his hand. He tries to play it casual as he pops off the top, shakes two pills onto the bar, picks them up and washes them down with his straight bourbon, then tucks the bottle back into his jacket.

"Vitamins," he tells me. "Have to take them every day."

But I've seen it—seen the shape of the pills in his hand, just before he popped them. That telltale blue pill, diamond-shaped. He knows I'm going to let him fuck me.

He smiles, lifting his glass. "Here's a toast to you, Erica. The most beautiful girl I've ever met."

The fantasy requires that I be reluctant, but now I'm so turned on I couldn't stop myself even if I really did want to. I've let my hand drift up to Hal's crotch, let my fingers curve around the shaft of his cock through his pants. The pills have made him hard all the way—hard, and large. He's got quite a big cock, and I know where I'm going to take it.

The final marker has been passed. As I finish my drink, he puts his fingers gently on my face and turns me toward him. I part my lips. Hal kisses me, his tongue forcing its way whiskey-sweet into my mouth, his hand moving down to mine and pressing it hard against the shaft of his cock. His other hand, around my back, pulls me close and slides up to grip my hair. He holds me tight as he forces my hand against his cock. His lips come off of mine and I pant, feeling as if I'm on a merry-go-round. My cunt aches as I lean forward to press it against the bar stool. Hal is going to fuck me. He's going to fuck me in all three of my holes.

"See what you've done to me?" he whispers. "Let's go

somewhere, Erica. I think you'd like that, wouldn't you?"

I'm breathing hard, gasping for air.

All I can do is nod.

Hal tosses a twenty on the bar, stands me up. He steadies me with his arm around my shoulders, his hand gripping my wrist tightly. His suit jacket brushes my nipples through the thin dress. Everyone in the restaurant looks at us as he walks me toward the door.

Moving down the long hotel corridor, I lean against him, unable to stand on my own. I can feel the wetness of my pussy dripping down my thighs. I try to keep them pressed together, but I'm already tottering on my high heels.

"Do—do you have a room?" I ask.

"No," he says, "but I know a nice romantic stairwell. A whore like you doesn't rate an expensive hotel room, anyway. No wonder your boyfriend dumped you."

Hal opens a heavy fire door and shoves me through. I stumble down half a flight. Hal grabs my arm and shoves me to my knees. I feel my stockings ripping as Hal grips my hair and tangles his fingers in it. He's got his pants open in an instant and before I know it he's leaning back against the wall, dragging me forward and forcing my mouth down onto his cock.

A surge goes through me as I taste it. The second I feel his hard cock in my mouth, all I feel is the hunger for cock that led me here tonight in the first place.

"Oh, yeah," says Hal. "Your boyfriend dumped you because you were a little cocksucker. You're good at it, too. How many cocks did you suck while you were going out with him, anyway? Just a drink or two and you're down on your knees, Erica. You're cheaper than the cheapest whore. You would have sucked me if I hadn't bought you *any* drinks, wouldn't you?"

I don't even try to answer, since he already knows what I would say; all I can feel is Hal's cock pushing its way down my throat, his hand in my hair guiding me up and down. His cock is huge, long and thick, almost too thick for me to swallow. But I've had a lot of practice, and I manage to take his cock down my throat, my gag reflex ruined by all the alcohol. The stairwell spins around me as I bob up and down on his cock, moaning softly, feeling my cunt wet. *He's going to fuck me*, I think. *He's going to fuck me in my cunt.*

And then he's going to fuck me in the ass.

Hal pulls me off his cock, turns my head up toward him. I can feel the strings of drool running down my chin.

"You want my come down your throat, Erica?"

"Please…" I gasp, my mouth open wide, sticky spit glistening between my mouth and Hal's cock.

"You want it? You want to eat my come?"

"Please fuck me," I gasp. "Please…"

"You want me to fuck that sweet pussy of yours?" he growls.

"Fuck me…in…the…"

"What?"

I finally manage to choke it out. "Fuck me in the ass," I whimper, and tears fill my eyes. Hal chuckles and shoves me down onto my hands and knees. I stay there doggie-style while he reaches down and yanks my skirt up.

"You're still wearing your clothes," he tells me. "Underwear and all. Strip everything off."

My hands shaking, I begin to wriggle out of my dress. It comes off over my head, and I push it into a ball in the corner of the stairwell. Hal unhitches my bra and it falls forward, revealing my breasts.

"Panties, too," says Hal. "But not the stockings. Or the shoes."

The panties are under the garter belt; as I obediently begin to pull them down, Hal realizes this and I hear the click of his pocket knife. He slits the thin strings of my thong and pulls the soaked, ruined garment out from between my legs.

Still standing over me, he gets his hands between my thighs and forces my legs wide apart. His hand on my pussy makes me gasp, and he knows in an instant just how wet I am for his cock.

That's when I hear the fire door opening overhead, half a flight up. I look up and see the busboy—the one who couldn't stop refilling my water. He looks at me, shocked—not knowing what to think.

"Just what you need, Erica," says Hal. "Another cock to fill you. Get down here." He says something in Spanish, and I see the busboy smile as he comes down the stairs toward me.

Oh, god. It's happening.

He unzips his pants and pulls out his cock as Hal takes his place behind me. Hal's cock nudges open my lips, making me shudder as he pushes his cock, still wet with my spittle, against my clit. I almost come right then, but I'm distracted by the feel of the busboy's hand tangled in my hair. He lifts my face onto his cock and forces my lips around the head.

I start to suck it, obediently accepting every inch of the shaft until it forces its way into my throat. Fucked wide by Hal's cock, my throat opens for the busboy, and he starts to fuck my face roughly as Hal positions his cock at my entrance.

Then Hal drives into me fiercely, quickly—not caring if he's going too fast. He shoves his cock in until the head strikes my cervix, and I utter a grunt deep in my throat. But the busboy's cock keeps me from screaming, or even moaning. Hal begins to fuck me.

As his cock slides into my aching pussy, I feel his thumb nuzzling between my cheeks. He pushes it in and I tense as he violates my asshole. But the busboy won't let me up; he's gripping my hair tight, forcing me up and down on his cock. Forcing me to suck him. Hal works his thumb deep into my ass and draws it around in big circles, opening me up for his cock. *He's going to fuck me in the ass*, I keep thinking, trying to prepare myself for the invasion of his cock. It's big, and I don't know if I can take it.

The terror rushes through me as Hal slides his cock out of my sopping pussy and presses it between my cheeks. He doesn't go slow, doesn't wait to see if I'm ready for him. He just shoves it into my ass, and a big strangled yelp bursts from my lungs, stopped dead by the thickness of the busboy's cock filling my throat.

There's a moment of pain as his cock violates my asshole; then the pleasure starts to flow through me. You've ruined me. You've planned all this to hurt me, to humiliate me. You know I come whenever you fuck my ass. You know I come easier from being fucked in the ass than from anything else.

You know I'm going to come on Hal's cock.

The busboy fucks faster into my throat, using my face. I open wide for him, feeling my orgasm thundering toward me as Hal uses my ass. I come just an instant before he does, and he knows—I can tell he knows—even though I can't make a peep, forced quiet by the busboy's cock. Once I've let myself go, feeling the pleasure explode through me, there's only a moment of soaring on my orgasm before Hal comes too, his hot come filling my ass, stinging it. And then the busboy pulls out, grabs my face, forces my mouth open wide with one hand and grabs my hand with the other. He wraps my fingers around his cock and I obediently start to stroke. "Stick out your tongue, bitch." When the first stream hits the back of my throat I moan and open wide for it; more streams follow, hot jism filling my mouth, splashing across my cheeks, covering my chin.

I slump forward on my hands and knees, my breath coming in huge panting sobs. Hal pulls out of my ass and zips up. The busboy also tucks his cock away.

"I don't think your boyfriend will want you back now," Hal says contemptuously as he mounts the stairs. The busboy follows him. Hal pauses outside the fire door. I look over my shoulder at him, still spread on hands and knees, my ass leaking come and my face covered with it, my pussy still aching from my intense orgasm.

"You forgot this in the bar," he says, and tosses the key card at me. It hits the landing with a snap. "Though I bet your boyfriend's already changed the lock."

Hal and the busboy disappear through the fire door, letting it slam behind them.

I pick myself up, limbs shaking, head still spinning from all the alcohol. I can't find my bra, and my panties are nothing but ruined, stripped fabric. I wriggle into my tiny dress, well aware that without a bra it shows my tits to anyone who will look. I don't even bother to wipe the come off my face, or try to dab it off my spread cheeks. I just let it run down the backs of my thighs as I sway down the stairs looking for the right floor. I can barely walk after all those drinks and the rough treatment Hal forced on me. I bend over and take off my high-heeled shoes and walk down flight after flight wearing nothing on my feet but my shredded, ruined stockings, great holes ripped in the knees where I genuflected before first Hal's cock, then the busboy's.

I look like a well-used whore.

I finally make it to the right floor, stumble through the fire door. No one is in the hallway, thank god. I find the right hotel room and put the key in the door. The light flashes red at first, then red again, and I feel a wave of panic. You've abandoned me.

The third time, the light goes green and I push the door open, fall into the hotel room.

You catch me in your arms, pulling me into darkness. You carry me over to the bed, but before you can lay me down I'm on my knees again, feeling the plush hotel carpet against my now bare knees. You're wearing only an expensive complimentary bathrobe and I've got it open in an instant, your cock in my mouth, my lips gliding hungrily up and down the shaft as you caress the back of my head.

"It looks like Steve treated you right."

It was filled with surprises, this night. Not the general facts, but the specifics. The details tipped me off before we even got to the restaurant. The three lubricating suppositories you told me to put in my ass before we went out. The fact that "Hal," or Steve, as I knew him when we played together, had grayed his normally black hair and put on a suit. The fact that the restaurant you took me to was the one where Mark worked as a busboy, having earned the indulgence of his manager just enough to slip away for a quick scene in the stairwell.

It was risky, to be sure. Mark could have lost his job. Who knows; if someone had happened along at the wrong instant, they both might have been arrested for rape—though there would be little chance of my pressing charges, since it was all my idea. Since I begged for it, begged you to set this up, begged you to make sure everything went perfectly. And it did.

It was risky, but so worth it.

I tell you that with every stroke of my mouth on your cock, every little whimper I give as I suck you.

"Thank you, baby," I sigh, my lips sliding off your cock. "Thank you so much."

"Don't mention it," you tell me, and seize my head roughly, twisting my hair in your hand.

House Rules

SARA DEMUCI

"Come on," Michael said, loud into my ear so I could hear him over the music. "You *can't* pass this up!"

And I didn't want to. Michael and I had come to the fetish ball knowing there would be a cordoned-off play area; we'd even joked about the possibility that we might play in it. But I hadn't expected it to be so crowded—every piece of equipment packed tight with players, and the bar behind the cordons crammed even tighter with spectators.

But Michael and I had found a place to sequester ourselves so we could watch this one beautiful mistress play with a gorgeous, muscled young stud as we swayed to the pounding trance beat. She'd had him bent over the spanking bench and was flogging his ass. I'd gotten quite wet watching them, and Michael had been behind me, cradling me in his arms, so I had been able to feel quite clearly that Michael was as turned on as I was.

Now, the mistress had finished with the young stud and sent him away.

And she was looking right at me and crooking her finger.

She was breathtaking—with a gorgeous, aquiline face; long dark hair and a slim body packed into a tight corset; G-string and high-heeled boots. She had a flogger in one hand and a paddle in the other, and she was unquestionably summoning me, though I couldn't have heard her say a word.

Michael knows how much I love to be spanked, but I'd never been flogged before. My knees went weak as I looked at the mistress and made a "Me!?" sort of gesture. She gave me the most intense bedroom eyes I've ever seen, and I melted.

Michael pushed me gently toward her. I walked forward as if in a dream.

Then the mistress snapped her fingers and pointed right at Michael.

"Him, too," she mouthed, her words shrouded by the music.

We passed the safety monitor and went into the cordoned-off play area. It was crowded, but the mistress had cleared a tidy space no one dared violate. I hadn't even thought about the fact that we couldn't negotiate if we couldn't hear each other—and that turned me on even more. What was I walking into?

She had to bend forward and talk right into my ear, loud, to be heard over the music. "I'm Xenia," she shouted.

"Lisa," I told her.

Michael didn't say a word.

"I'm going to play with you, Lisa," shouted Mistress Xenia. "Do you like to be spanked? Flogged?"

"J—just spanked," I shouted nervously.

She nodded, put her lips close to my ear. "Then that's what you'll get."

I nodded back at her, my pussy feeling hot as Mistress Xenia ran her hands down my side, playing with the way my lace-trimmed PVC G-string met my garter belt. She spread her palm and drew it over my shimmering bustier, feeling my nipples poke through it.

She put her hand on my shoulder and moved me out of the way so she could lean over and talk into Michael's ear. When she pulled away, Michael took hold of my shoulders and Mistress Xenia took my hand. They guided me toward the spanking bench, and I saw Mistress Xenia nod to someone, who brought over a chair.

Mistress Xenia pushed me down over the spanking bench while Michael took the chair.

Then he pushed my face into his lap and started to stroke my hair.

Mistress Xenia circled my wrists with buckling restraints and clipped them to the side of the spanking bench. Now I was helpless; I couldn't get free if I wanted to. I struggled against the bonds, getting more and more turned on. I shivered as I felt Mistress Xenia's hands running over my ass. She slapped the insides of my thighs and I obediently spread my legs, leaning heavily on the bench. I felt her bending down behind me, putting leather restraints around my ankles, too. She fastened my ankles spread wide, forcing me to keep my legs open for her.

The first blow came with her open hand, right on my sweet spot. She was pressed up to my side, embracing me tightly as she started to spank me. The nearness of her body made me tingle. She spanked me again. And again, softly, softly, then harder, building up pressure as I raised my ass into the air for her. She could tell I liked it—it was making me so wet. I love nothing more than being spanked, and I could feel the blows of Mistress Xenia's hand reverberating right into my pussy.

Michael was excited, too; I could feel his hard cock against my face. I was so turned on I would have done anything. But I never expected to do what I did.

As Mistress Xenia spanked me, Michael unbuckled his belt and unzipped his pants.

Then he took out his cock and guided my mouth onto it.

I felt a stab of fear—there were strict prohibitions against sexual activity. What about the house rules? Was the monitor watching? Was the *crowd* watching? Even over the music, I could hear them clapping and cheering. They *were* watching. Everyone crowded around could see me sucking my husband's cock. Everyone could see me bent over, ass in the air, Michael's beautiful cock sliding between my lips as I bobbed up and down on it.

I wriggled my ass and Mistress Xenia spanked me harder.

I could feel my pussy throbbing as I sucked Michael's cock. I was incredibly wet, and Michael knew it. Mistress Xenia knew it, too. I moaned as I felt her hand on my pussy. That was forbidden, too. She plucked the G-string out of the way and started to rub my cunt, feeling how wet I was. Then, the crotch of the G-string tucked to the side leaving my pussy exposed, she spanked me again. Harder. Right on my sweet spot, making my bare cunt ache each time. She pushed her body up against me. This couldn't be happening. This was like every one of my fantasies, but it wasn't allowed—was it?

Michael held my hair up behind my head so the crowd could see me suck him. So they could see his long, hard cock sliding between my lips as I struggled against the four-point restraints.

But Mistress Xenia had more things in mind for me.

I felt her fingers on my cunt, probing me, and I was embarrassed at how wet I was. We hadn't negotiated this; she didn't know I would be okay with it. Why did she do it, then? Maybe because she could tell I wanted something more?

She slid her fingers into me—first two fingers, then three—and started to slowly fuck my cunt.

I squealed and tried to pull away, but Michael and the restraints held me, and I surrendered, letting Mistress Xenia fuck me as I serviced him. But then her fingers slipped out of me, and I was afraid she might have been asked to stop. *Please. No. Please don't stop.*

But Michael didn't stop. He kept guiding my head up and down on his cock, and the taste of his pre-come was like ambrosia. I suckled at it hungrily as I wondered where Mistress Xenia was.

Then I felt her body pressing up against mine. Her thighs against mine. Her hands on my hips.

Her cock at my entrance.

I could feel the roughness of the straps. She was going to fuck me. She had gone away because she was putting on her strap-on.

She teased my cunt open with the thick head of her cock. I moaned and fought violently against the restraints as she entered me—the struggle excited me more. That made the crowd cheer louder.

When she entered me, I came—right away. I felt her cock sliding into me, and my whole body convulsed in orgasm. Michael could tell; he pulled my head up and listened to me moan. I let myself go, totally, moaning and screaming so loud everyone could hear me even over the music. Then as Mistress Xenia started fucking me harder, my loud moans turned into soft ones; my pussy was so sensitive now, after my orgasm, and I wanted more, wishing I could reach back and open my pussy wide for her cock. But I was bound, and as I struggled against the bonds I only felt my pleasure heightening.

Michael guided my mouth back onto his cock, and I started sucking him in earnest, wanting his come.

Mistress Xenia reached under me and rubbed my clit, hard, not warming me up—knowing I didn't *need* any warm-up. She rubbed so hard that for an instant I wanted her to stop—and then she fucked me deeper, all the way into my cunt, filling me, and I wanted her to never, ever stop. I wriggled my butt back and forth and pulled hard against the restraints, making the whole spanking bench shake. That only made her pound me harder as she rubbed my clit in little circles, faster, faster, faster as her hips forced her cock into me again and again.

I came again, even harder than before, but this time my moans weren't audible to the crowd—because my mouth and throat were filled with Michael's cock.

I felt the first spasm of his long shaft and tasted the bitterness I so loved. Just a hint, at first, which made me suck him harder, bob my head up and down faster. Then a thick pulse of come filled my mouth and I moaned and gulped, wanting it all. His hips ground against me as my lips clamped around his shaft and he filled my mouth with his juice. I drank it all, not spilling a drop, wishing it could go on forever.

My head was spinning; I was so high on endorphins I felt like I was in another world. Mistress Xenia unbuckled the restraints as I covered Michael's softening cock with tiny licks, wanting to taste it as long as I could.

Michael fastened his pants and the two of them helped me off the spanking bench. Mistress Xenia still wore her cock, and I wanted to get down on my knees and suck that one, too. She pressed her mouth to mine and kissed me deeply.

Then she kissed Michael, too, and pressed a card into his hand.

She put her lips to my ear and spoke just loud enough for me to hear her over the pulsing music.

"Next time," she said, "we play without *any* house rules."

Her hand gently squeezed my ass, making my pussy quiver.

Rest Stop
FELIX D'ANGELO

I pulled up outside the rest stop, right by the men's room. I put the car in park and turned it off. Steevi looked at me nervously.

I smiled at her.

"You know what I have in mind," I said.

She shook her head. "I'm...I'm not sure, Sir."

"Make a guess."

She looked at the entrance to the men's room, at the dilapidated door hanging off its hinges. "You...you want me to go in there," she said. Her face was flushing deep red. Her nipples stood out clearly in the tight white minidress she wore. She plucked nervously at the hem of the minidress, trying in vain to pull it down more than an inch past her crotch. Her thighs were bare, her knees shrouded in the knee pads I'd had her purchase just yesterday at the sporting goods store. I could almost see her pussy, and I knew it wasn't protected by hair or panties. I kept her bare, exposed, vulnerable. I could see her nipples becoming more evident as they got harder. Her face flushed deeper red, and I could see her cleavage getting pinker.

"Good guess," I told her. "And then what?"

"I...I don't know," she said.

"Make a guess," I said, reaching out to caress the thick knee pads she wore.

"You want me to get down on my knees."

"And?"

She hesitated, looking down at the ground. I leaned over, reached between her legs. She obediently opened them, making the hem of her dress ride up above her pussy so I could see it. When I drew my fingers up her slit, I found it incredibly wet. I slipped my fingers into her, making her moan. When I drew them out, I put them to her mouth and she obediently licked them clean.

"And suck cock," she said.

"That's right," I said. "About midnight, this rest stop gets hopping. It's the only rest stop on this road with a men's room that doesn't get locked at night, because every time they lock it people just break the door off the hinges. Straight guys come here every night to get their dicks sucked by other straight guys. Think it'll be a big thrill for them to get a woman's mouth on their cocks?"

My hand went back between her legs, and I caressed her juice-slick clit. She moaned. Her arousal was obvious, and when I kissed her she was hungry, her mouth sucking at my tongue as I savaged her. When I pulled back, she smiled, trying hard not to display her fear.

"Yes," she said. "I think it'll be a great thrill."

"Then get in there," I said. "Your boyfriends will start showing up soon."

She hesitated, obviously toying with the idea of using her safeword. She always has that option, but in our two years together Steevi has never used it more than once in a given month. I push her as far as she'll go, always knowing that she'll stop me if she absolutely has to.

But she so rarely does.

Steevi opened the car door, got out, and walked toward the men's room, tugging down the hem of her minidress.

"Take the center stall," I told her.

She looked back at me, her nipples standing clear in the light of my headlights. She looked glorious in the tiny dress, her firm body wrapped tightly and exposed for all to see. Except there was no one to see it—yet.

Steevi turned and headed toward the darkened door.

When she disappeared into the darkness of the men's room, I killed the headlights, pulled my laptop out of the back, and set it up on the seat Steevi had occupied. I booted up and fired up the software that would show me the scene captured by the wireless infrared camera and microphone I'd installed earlier that afternoon. It had cost quite a pretty penny to get one of that kind of quality, but it was worth it.

I had placed the tiny camera immediately above the two bathroom stalls, allowing me to see both of them from directly above. Steevi had to know I was watching. I'd used this trick before, though never with such edgy certainty. She'd sucked strangers, but she'd never done it in such inglorious environs.

I could feel my cock hardening in my pants.

The fact that this was the most deserted stretch of highway in the state, and that our friends would be traveling a hundred or more miles to reach it, did little to lessen my arousal. After all, you never knew when a stranger might happen by—a real stranger, not one of the men Steevi and I played with regularly. And you might see a cop uniform that wasn't bought at a leather shop on Santa Monica Boulevard.

But everything else about this was perfectly planned. Steevi would know each cock in her mouth, but she wouldn't know she knew—not until she tasted it, and maybe not even then. After all, I liked to find new partners for her, and part of her own fantasy was that she never knew when a brand-new, unfamiliar cock would find its way into her mouth.

Steevi had closed and latched the men's room stall. She must have gotten the picture as soon as she saw the glory holes smashed out of the panels on each side of her center stall. She knew she'd be taking on two dates at once. With the stall door latched, she lowered herself onto her knees and waited, her face up against one of the glory holes.

About eleven-forty-five, another car pulled into the lot—a big pickup truck with a beefy, flannel-clad guy driving. He looked me over, as if to make sure I wasn't a cop. Maybe he thought I was a guy waiting to go in and give head. Either way, he disappeared into the bathroom.

Almost immediately another car pulled up, this one a sedan. There were three young guys in it, out for a thrill, and they joked and teased each other about being faggots as they got out of the car and headed into the bathroom. Our friends, getting into the act even more than I expected.

I watched, everything illuminated in reddish-gray by the infrared camera. The beefy guy was first. It was almost pitch black inside the bathroom, so he mustn't have known he was about to get sucked off by a woman. He stepped into the stall and unzipped his pants, took out his cock and took a long, luxurious piss, a thick stream hitting the toilet as the teenage guys crowded into the bathroom. Without even shaking off very well, he turned and shoved his cock through the glory hole. It connected with Steevi's face, a face I'd fucked so many delicious times before. Steevi didn't hesitate; she wrapped her lips around the guy's cockhead and started bobbing up and down, servicing him.

The three young men crowded into the other stall, pushing and shoving each other as they argued over who was going to be first. Finally one pulled out his cock and stuck it through the hole.

Steevi reached behind her and took hold of it, getting it hard as she sucked off the beefy guy.

His hips started to pump, fucking Steevi's face as she got her next cock ready. I admired the way her mouth worked up and down on his shaft, one hand milking his balls while the other stroked the next guy hard. From what I could see the beefy flannel guy had a good-sized cock, but Steevi took it all, no doubt swallowing it down her throat. Within minutes the guy let out a long, low sigh and Steevi clamped her lips around his shaft. I knew she was swallowing.

The guy zipped up, left the stall. One of the young men heard him leaving and took his place. By the time he put his hard cock through the hole, Steevi had turned around and knelt to suck his friend's cock. She was going at it fiercely, but she heard the other guy's footsteps and reached behind her to keep him ready as she sucked off his buddy.

The first one came almost immediately—premature ejaculation, no doubt. Steevi stayed down low on his cock until he'd pumped her mouth full. Then she turned around and her hand guided the new boy's cock into her mouth. She started to suck.

Two more cars pulled up. I was too fixated on the screen at first to notice who was in them, but when I glanced up I saw that there were several guys in each car. They crowded into the bathroom. I looked back on the screen. Steevi finished up with the second teenager and moved on to the third as the new men crammed into the bathroom stalls and took out their cocks.

Someone finally noticed the third hole I'd cut in the door of Steevi's stall. One of the guys, apparently less shy than the others, pushed his cock through the hole and Steevi obediently began stroking him off with one hand while she kept another cock hard with her other hand. Her mouth continued to work on the third young stud until he groaned and shot in her mouth.

Steevi looked straight up and swallowed, her eyes wide. Did she know I was watching? Despite the poor resolution of the infrared camera, I could see the glistening on her chin from the faint lights through the window. Her face was covered in come. She was drooling it.

More men crowded into the stalls, waiting their turn to get sucked through the glory hole. Steevi obediently moved from one to the other, using her hands to keep the others hard and ready so she would waste no time when her mouth finally got to them.

I timed several of the men with the clock showing in the bottom right corner of the laptop's screen and found it was less than three minutes from the moment Steevi's mouth touched their cockheads to the moment she drew her lips off of them, dribbling semen. They flooded out of the bathroom door and jumped into their cars, the ones who came in groups slapping each other on the back at the free blow job they'd just gotten.

Then I felt my heart in my throat. I looked up to see a pair of black sedans pulling into the rest stop parking lot. At first I panicked—until I realized these weren't unmarked police cars at all. They were rentals, and the uniformed "cops" inside were supposed to be here.

There were four cops total. They adjusted their belts as they walked past me. One of them nodded. I knew him well, of course—but he still looked mighty intimidating in uniform.

Steevi had almost finished the men in the bathroom— a total of twelve so far. There were two men left waiting to have their cocks sucked. They were too distracted to notice the cops. One of the men stood with Steevi's mouth wrapped around the base of his shaft, working hungrily; the other with Steevi's delicate, long-nailed hand stroking him into readiness for her mouth.

She swallowed one man's load and moved on to the other. The one zipped up and pushed past the cops, nodding to them.

Two "cops" crowded into the vacant stall. One took his place behind the guy getting his cock sucked, waiting for the glory hole. The other unzipped and put his cock through the third glory hole. Steevi reached out and took it, stroking him hard as she finished the cock she was on, swallowing eagerly.

The guy pulled back, zipped up, and nervously pushed past the cops, running for the door.

Steevi didn't even know they were "cops." But I did, and it made my cock throb even harder than before. In the gray-pink light of the infrared I could see when she stretched her head back to massage her sore jaw that her eyes were closed.

One cop unzipped and put his hard cock through the vacant glory hole. The other two grabbed the hole and punched it, cracking it wider until it was oblong enough to fit them both at once. Steevi faced four cocks.

She took one cock in each hand and started sucking the first cop's. He groaned as her lips eagerly worked up and down on his shaft.

It was only a minute before he came. Steevi missed some of his come, dribbling it down her chin and onto her breasts, soaking the thin minidress she wore. She kept reaching behind her to stroke one cop's dick and turned her attention to the oblong glory hole that offered two.

She went from one cock to the other. One cop reached through the hole and grabbed her hair, guiding his cock into her mouth at the same time as his friend's. The two of them fucked Steevi's face at the same time as her hand twisted behind her to keep their fellow cop hard and ready for her.

Both cops shot at once, filling her mouth with their semen as she groaned and gurgled deep in her throat. Semen ran down her chin and soaked her dress. Her hair was matted with it.

She licked them clean; they pulled out, zipped up, and went to wait in their "cruiser."

Steevi turned to take care of the last cop. Her head bobbed

up and down on him, and he reached through the glory hole to hold her face so he could face-fuck her better. Steevi moaned as he pumped her. It wasn't long before he came in her mouth and she swallowed.

The cop buckled his belt, zipped his pants, and left.

The two cruisers pulled out of the parking lot; no other cars showed up. The cop cars had probably scared them away.

Steevi stayed on her knees, her face against the glory hole, dripping come. I left the laptop on the seat, locked the car, and went inside.

I had to break the latch to force the stall door, but I moved fast enough that I don't think Steevi was sure it was me. I pushed her over the toilet and she leaned hard on the pipes as I pulled up her short dress and forced her legs open. She lifted her ass in the air as I pulled my rock-hard dick out and shoved it into her.

She was gushing. Juice ran down her legs as I entered her.

I started fucking her, pushing down on her ass to keep her low so I could hit her G-spot just right. I knew how to make her come, and I knew any residual doubts about whether she wanted this would be shattered in her own mind by the explosion of an orgasm. I pushed one hand into her mouth, smearing the streams of semen all over her lips, and grabbed her hair with the other, pulling her head back so she had to lean hard against me as I pounded into her.

She let out a great gasping moan and I felt her cunt contracting around my shaft. She was coming, and she didn't even try to hide it. She let out great sobs of release as I fucked her, and I knew that now was the time to drive my dominance home.

I pulled out of her cunt and yanked her skirt up higher, moving my cockhead between her cheeks.

"No," she gasped. "N—no—no!" But she didn't call out her safeword, didn't do the one thing she knew, beyond a doubt, would put an end to the scene.

I drove into her hard in one thrust, taking her ass and making her squeal with surprise. I pushed her hard against the toilet pipes, listening to her sob and shudder as I fucked her dry hole.

"Rub your clit," I growled.

"N—no!" she gasped. "P—please!"

"Rub it!"

She reached between her legs so quickly I knew her protest had just been a resistance to the ultimate humiliation of coming a second time. She began to rub her clit eagerly as I fucked her ass, my hand in the small of her back keeping her steady as I pounded into her. I was fighting not to shoot my load; her incredibly tight ass always made me come so quickly. But I managed to hold off as I took her anally, making her rub herself to the second orgasm I knew she so badly wanted.

"Oh, god," she sobbed. "Don't make me—oh!"

Then she came, and the spasms of her asshole around my cock were even stronger than those of her first orgasm. She kept rubbing violently, bringing herself off until I wasn't sure if she'd come twice more or three times more, one after the other as she did sometimes when she was really, really turned on. It was all I needed to let myself go, pounding my cock into her ass and erupting in a flood of semen deep inside her. I groaned, letting her know that I was going off inside her, and as I did she pushed her ass back against me, demanding my load, and I knew she felt the flood of hot liquid as I injected her with my come.

"Th—thank you," she whimpered. "Thank you...."

I pulled out, tucked my cock away just like the others. Zipped up and turned to leave the bathroom.

I was already in the car before Steevi followed me, tottering on unsteady legs. Her dress was torn, the neckline opened so I could see one pink nipple hanging out as her white skin shone in the headlights. She swayed on her high heels and came to the side of the car, leaning up against the window, panting.

I reached over and unlocked the door. She stumbled as she pulled it open, leaning hard on the door and tumbling into the seat. I barely got the laptop out of the way.

She curled up in the passenger seat, her face dripping semen, her eyes wide and glazed.

"Thank you," she whimpered. "Thank you."

I started the car, put it in reverse, and pulled out of the parking lot.

On the long drive home, Steevi dropped off to sleep, her tit still hanging out, her dress still pulled up and semen running down the backs of her thighs. I pulled over to the side of the road and repositioned her so I could put on her seat belt.

I looked into her sleeping face, slick with other men's come, her hair matted with it.

It had been hard for me. For every aspect of it that had turned me on, there had been jealousy, rage, confusion. But when it came right down to it, I loved her. And she had begged me, in page after page of her diary, detailing this, her fondest fantasy for more years than she could count.

The diary she had pleaded with me to read, whispering to me that I had permission to do anything—*anything*—she'd written about in it. How could I let her down?

Steevi began to snore softly, delicately, as I pulled back onto the interstate and headed for home.

Daddy's Boy
Elizabeth Colvin

"Come on, boy. Come over here and tell Daddy how much you appreciate his hospitality."

I take the cigar out of my mouth and smile at him.

Lounging in the armchair, I reach down and unzip my leather pants. I pull out my cock and start stroking it. My boy looks at the big, thick shaft of my cock and licks his lips.

Then he goes down on his knees and plants his mouth on the head of my cock. He takes my shaft into his mouth until the head nudges the top of his throat. Then, without hesitating, he swallows, forcing the shaft down his throat without even a hint of a gag reflex. That sends a shudder through my body; I can feel my pussy aching. He starts working on my cock, sucking it like an expert.

I don't look much like any daddy I've ever known. The tight leather pants, big black boots, and Harley Davidson T-shirt could belong to a daddy, sure. But there's no disguising my broad hips or the way the pants hang so low on them, revealing my flowery tattoos and my navel ring. And I haven't strapped down my tits, which are big enough to stretch the T-shirt and, even with a sports bra underneath, show my nipples as they get hard in response to the sight and feel of my boy's mouth on my cock.

But it doesn't matter, because I'm a daddy; I've got the big, thick cock to prove it. Silicone, yes; maybe not as sensitive as a real daddy's cock. With this daddy's cock, it's not just a matter of licking and sucking around the head or teasing the underside of the shaft. Sucking this cock is a lot more work. My boy has to push and work his head around and suck my cock harder, pushing the base of the dildo against my clit to make my pussy throb in response. But I don't care and my boy doesn't care, either, because my boy knows I'm his daddy. I've got the cock to prove it—and the armchair.

And a boy is exactly what he is, tonight. Torn jeans, so faded they're almost white, hug his lithe body, showing off the big bulge in his pants, swept to the right and getting bigger as he sucks me. His tight white T-shirt, so tight it's almost see-through, shows off his perfect chest. He looks like some boy hustler I picked up on the street, offered a place to stay in return for a blow job. The big white athletic shoes are a decidedly adolescent touch.

The whole package makes my pussy so wet I can hardly stand it.

And when he looks up at me with his mouth around my cock, there's no question that this is my boy, servicing me.

"Come on, boy, suck it better than that. Earn your keep."

He launches more eagerly into it, his mouth pumping

up and down on my cock and forcing it deeper into his throat. He's obviously a skilled cocksucker; he doesn't even hesitate when the head of my cock presses against his throat. He just swallows, knowing that's what I want. I want to feel him take it all the way, feeling it in his belly, just like he will when I put it up his ass.

His eyes turn back up to me and I grin down at him, flicking ash off the end of the cigar. "I think it's time you sucked a little ass, boy."

I pull him off of my cock and turn around on the armchair, pulling my leather pants down over my hips. When I've got them down around my knees, I bend over, pushing my ass out for him. He leans in and obediently presses his face between my cheeks, his tongue sliding into my ass. I have to stifle a gasp that I know will sound way too feminine, and I barely manage to replace it with a manly grunt as I reach back behind me to grab his hair and push his face more firmly into my ass. His tongue works its way deeper into my asshole. He alternates between teasing the entrance with big long swirls of his tongue and pushing hard into it like he's fucking me with that limber little organ. I want to reach down and rub my clit; I want to come so bad it's driving me crazy. But instead of rubbing my clit I reach down and begin to jerk off, stroking my cock, pumping it hard up and down, and that only makes me want to come even more. When I push the dildo down I can feel the base against my clit, almost direct enough to make me come, but not quite. God, I want to fuck him so bad.

I'm so turned on I can hardly speak. But I manage it, barely, working hard to maintain a gruff rumble in my voice instead of a girly squeak. I turn my head and look down at him over my shoulder. He's beautiful, his mouth planted between my cheeks, licking me. His eyes are turned up toward me, and I look into them as I growl at him.

"You take it up the ass, boy?"

His mouth comes away from my ass and he says, "If I have to, Daddy."

"You have to, boy," I tell him.

He moves back and I get off the armchair, still stroking my cock. I watch as he shucks his white T-shirt, showing off his beautiful chest. I run my hand down it, working my cock faster. He unzips his jeans and peels them off, kicking his way out of his white athletic shoes. He's not wearing socks. I look at his gorgeous cock, standing there hard, the tip glistening.

"You can suck it if you want," he says weakly, not meeting my eyes.

I grab his hair and pull his face close to mine.

"No kissing," he says, sounding petulant and whiny. "I don't do that. I'm not a faggot."

The sound of that helpless plea sends a new surge of arousal through my pussy and into my cock. I've got him right where I want him.

Ignoring his protest, I press my lips to his and thrust my tongue into his mouth. He lets me for a moment, then begins to respond with his own tongue against mine. I kiss him deeper, then spin him around and shove him against the armchair. He climbs onto it, knees pressed to the thick, padded arms, legs spread, ass in the air. He reaches back and parts his cheeks as I grab the bottle of lube on the end table.

I pour lube between his cheeks and work two fingers into his ass—not even bothering to start with one. He gasps as I penetrate him, and I reach between his legs to feel his cock pulsing with excitement.

"You like that, boy? You like taking it up the ass?"

"If I have to, Daddy," he says nervously.

"You have to, boy," I tell him. "You have to like it. And I know you're going to."

I add some lube to the head of my cock and push his back down till he's crouched down low and his ass is in the right position. I nuzzle the head of my cock against his tight entrance. His ass opens right up as I thrust into it; he lets out a shuddering gasp as I drive it in to the hilt.

I start to fuck him; for some reason, this position pushes the base of the dildo against my clit at just the right angle. Or maybe fucking my boy in the ass just turns me on more than anything. I reach up and grab his hair, listening to him moan as I shove my cock roughly into his ass, each thrust harder, building up speed.

His hand is underneath him, pumping his cock. His hips start to work, pushing him onto my cock. It's like he's trying to get it over with at first—then, as his hand quickens on his cock, like he wants it. He shoves hard onto me, his ass opening wider as it engulfs my cock. I pull his hair, making him squeal. At one point I reach down and spank his ass, which makes him fuck back onto me with even more urgency.

I don't even feel it coming, really. I've been working the dildo into him, pressing the base against my clit for so long that when I finally reach the breaking point I barely know it. It happens when he lets out a little whimper and I feel his body shaking—he's coming, shooting his load all over Daddy's armchair. I start to fuck him harder, faster, as his lips go slack and he leans hard against the back of the chair. I pound into him and that drives me over the top, my own orgasm sending my pussy and clit into tight spasms, my ass tightening as I feel the cooling moisture of my boy's spittle where he tongued me. I collapse on top of him and the chair groans under our combined weight as my body surges with pleasure, my high-pitched moans as feminine as it gets—but my boy doesn't seem to care.

He reaches back and strokes my hand where it still grips his hair. "Did my tight ass get you off real good, Daddy?"

"You have no idea," I said, still panting hard.

"Oh, I think I have some idea," he smiled, and squirmed around under me to hold me in his arms. He began to stroke my long hair gently and whispered, "Thank you, Daddy. Thanks for fucking me so good."

I curled up in my boy's embrace, sighing contentedly.

Medical Attention
SKYE BLACK

I woke up spread-eagled, stretched, helpless. I tried to move and
nothing happened. As my vision cleared, I saw myself in the
monitor facing the bed. I stared, disbelieving. My arms and legs
were in full-length casts, toes to crotch, fingers to shoulders,
all four limbs suspended with bolts through the sides of the
casts, heavy traction weights holding me immobile. I had been
forced into a giant *X* on the hospital bed, both my arms and
legs cocked just slightly at a wide angle. My head was shaved
and wrapped in thick white gauze and, under it, there was a
white plastic brace that attached to shiny metal prongs inserted
into the corners of my mouth. My belly was circled by a thick
off-white plastic brace with shiny aluminum struts attaching to
both my leg and arm casts. The brace went from my hips, just
above my crotch, to my chest just beneath my breasts.

And there was nothing covering those parts of me. Not
even a sheet. My breasts were bare, exposed on the big monitor

facing me. My crotch, also bare, had been shaved smooth, even the tiny dusting of pubic hair I usually wear having been denied me.

The traction spread my legs very wide.

I saw the winking red eye of the surveillance camera, the camera providing me the perfect view of myself. The monitor alternated between a full-body view of me, spread-eagled and immobilized, a close-up of my bare pussy, a close-up of my tits, and a close-up of my distressed, gauze-shrouded face.

I had been painted with makeup. Far from the deathly pallor that should haunt an accident victim, I had been given rosy cheeks with blush, thick eyelashes with mascara, bright blue eyelids with eye shadow. And, most arresting of all, I had been given full, accentuated lips with an intensely red shade of lipstick.

The monitor showed me my whore's painted face, then my breasts, then my pussy, up close. Then it showed all of me again, all of me, helpless and stock-still spread-eagled in the hospital bed.

The hospital door opened. A nurse in a starched white uniform came in. But the uniform dress was just a little too short, too tight on her rounded hips, the top cut just a little too close on her full breasts. Her white lace bra was visible under the low-cut top, which had a button or two undone. She was wearing makeup, too—lots of it.

"I see our patient's awake," she said. "How are you feeling, Mrs. Rubin?"

I murmured a wordless groan.

The nurse *tsked*. "Poor girl, doesn't remember a thing. Well, I'll let the doctor answer all your questions. He'll be here in a moment; I've got to get you ready for him, or there'll be hell to pay. He can be so demanding. I would hate to get in trouble with him. Now, be a good girl and take your medication, won't you?"

The nurse produced a small paper cup of pills. "Do you have to use the restroom?" she asked.

I nodded, and she sighed. "All right, well, let's do that first," she said. She took a plastic urinal from a nearby table, positioned herself between my spread legs, and tucked it just under my crotch.

But before she pressed it there, she took a moment to slide her fingers up the inside of my shaved pussy. It felt exquisitely sensitive, almost painfully so. She teased my lips apart, perhaps under the pretext of making sure I wouldn't dribble. Whatever it was, I didn't ask her, because the touch sent shivers through my immobilized body.

"My, my," she said, slipping her thumb into my pussy and making me gasp suddenly as a surge of pleasure erupted into me. "The patient is producing excessive lubrication. Clearly she likes looking at herself in the monitor. Don't be ashamed; many of our patients get very turned on looking at themselves. And I do understand it, Mrs. Rubin; you certainly make a pretty picture. You like seeing your pussy all clean like that, Mrs. Rubin? We had to shave it. The doctor insisted on it. And those tits of yours look much better bare. It's a shame you don't show them more often."

The nurse tipped the urinal cup to my crotch and said, "All right, go ahead."

My face reddened until it was crimson at the horror of having to pee in front of the nurse. I held back, despite the fact that my bladder was stretched full to the point of agony.

"Don't you dare hold back," said the nurse. "I won't have you going later, and making a mess for me or the other nurses to clean up. Now go, you filthy girl, and don't hold back a drop."

With a sigh, I let my bladder go, a steady stream filling the urinal. When I was finished, the nurse dabbed me with a paper towel and emptied the cup into the nearby sink.

"Good girl," she said. "Now, to prep you."

She pulled out a pair of bolts that held the bed; I realized that I was not on a normal hospital bed, but a breakaway bed that folded under, turning it into more of a gynecological exam table. It had to be custom-built. As she folded the bottom half of the bed away, I was left hanging with my ass just barely on the edge of the table and my legs spread wide and thrust up into the air. My cunt was now even more exposed than before. The nurse took a position next to me and bent down, looking into my face and smiling. She was so close that I could smell her perfume and the sweet scent of her breath.

Her hand traveled down my body and found my shaved pussy. She began to stroke me gently, rubbing my clit as my eyes went wider. My clit responded, growing harder as my pussy lubricated. Pleasure flowed into me and I resisted it as surely as I resisted the traction holding me still, but there was nothing I could do. Two fingers slid into me, telling the nurse just how wet she was making me. She drew firm circles around my clit with her wet fingers, and then drew back her hand and slapped my cunt.

I gasped; a strangled squeal came out of my mouth as she drew back and spanked my cunt again. She spanked harder, a third time, then a fourth, more rapidly, as I shuddered and moaned. Pleasure mingled with pain as she tortured my cunt.

"Clearly the patient likes it rough," she smiled as she paused in spanking my cunt. She then launched into it with new eagerness, slapping harder, faster, making my clit explode in sensation and making me mount toward orgasm. I fought off my climax even as it thundered toward me.

The doctor entered the room out of my field of vision; I couldn't even turn my head to see him. I lay there, displayed on the monitor, painted mouth spread wide open, body totally immobile, cunt being violently spanked as I was forced toward a climax, floating on cushions of sedated pleasure.

The nurse stopped. "The patient is prepped, Doctor."

"Start the recording."

"Yes, Doctor." The nurse produced a small tape recorder and held it out for the doctor to speak into as he came around between my legs. I tottered on the edge of orgasm, whimpering uncontrollably. I was so close I could feel it starting, my orgasm. Just a little bit would get me there.

The doctor's fingers slid into my pussy. I moaned, right on the edge. But he only gave me one smooth thrust, testing my wetness, and slid his hand up to test my clit. So close...but he didn't let me come.

"Patient presented with extreme vaginal lubrication," he said, businesslike, into the tape recorder. "And unusual swelling of the clitoris and nipples. Complete immobilization was recommended and performed."

As he spoke, the doctor unbuttoned his lab coat. I looked up at him through horny eyes, so turned on I couldn't even beg him for what I wanted.

"Vulvar assault by the attending nurse brought the patient

very close to orgasm, further indicating extreme arousal."

The nurse reached down and unzipped the doctor's pants.

"During examination, patient showed noticeable flushing of the chest, further distension of the nipples, and a sexual response to the sight of her own lips painted like a whore's." The nurse's hand disappeared inside the doctor's pants and pulled out his cock, naked and half-hard. She began to stroke it and it swelled as he talked. "Doctor's recommendation is for vaginal intercourse followed by anal penetration."

The nurse guided the doctor's cockhead to my exposed pussy, and I moaned as he entered me. The nurse held out the recorder, capturing his grunts as he began to thrust into me. His hands rested on my casts, as if keeping my legs spread—though there was no way I could have closed them, held as they were by the traction cables. He pounded into me roughly, fucking me so hard it made the hospital bed groan and creak. It was only a moment before I came, gasping.

"Primary orgasm was achieved three minutes after penetration," the doctor said, glancing at his watch. "Buildup to secondary orgasm began immediately."

The doctor plunged deep into my cunt and fucked me as I came. The sliding thrusts of his cock brought me down from orgasm, and I began to build toward a second one. As I did, I heard the snap of latex gloves and felt the nurse's gloved fingers prying open my cheeks even as the doctor kept thrusting into my cunt. Her fingers slid into my ass, slick with lube, and opened me up, first one finger, then two. More lube was added, and she forced a third finger into me.

"The patient is ready," said the nurse.

The doctor pulled his cock out of my pussy and let the

nurse position it at the entrance to my ass. My moans came even louder as he entered me again, this time forcing open my tight ass. I shuddered in the traction ropes and came again within moments. "Anal penetration produced a second orgasm in just over one minute. Oral semen to be administered now."

The doctor pulled out of my ass and took the tape recorder out of the nurse's hand. He came around the bed and positioned himself at my upper body. The nurse turned an unseen crank, lowering my head until my upper body was far enough below my hips to put my mouth within easy reach of the doctor's cock. Then she guided the doctor's cock to my mouth and began to stroke the shaft with her long, slim fingers as I opened wide, hungry for his come. The head hovered between my widespread lips, and the doctor groaned into the tape recorder as the first hot stream of come shot onto my tongue. I moaned and gulped it down, swallowing the next stream, and the next, overwhelmed by the pungent flavor of the doctor's come.

"Patient eagerly received administration of oral cumshot approximately fourteen minutes after initiation of vaginal intercourse. Condition of vaginal lubrication seems unchanged, but no further treatment recommended at this time."

The nurse tucked the doctor's cock back into his pants and buttoned up his lab coat. The doctor left without a word.

The nurse extended the lower half of the hospital bed again and unhitched the traction cables. She then pulled the Velcro straps on my hard breakaway casts and unbuckled the brace on my stomach. I moaned softly as she unwound the gauze from around my head. Laying there naked, no longer restrained, I could feel the spasms in my pussy that spelled the afterglow of two intense orgasms.

The nurse wiped down my thighs, my pussy, and dabbed away the lube that oozed out of my ass. She bent down and kissed me on the lips, smearing my lipstick.

"Thanks for visiting the Citadel," she said. "We hope you return soon."

I was too tired, exhausted, and dopey with codeine to answer. I just smiled up at her and gripped her hand.

"Take your time getting dressed," said the nurse. "Your husband will be waiting in the lobby. I'll try to make him comfortable."

She winked at me, and I sighed. It had been way too expensive, this fantasy of ours—after all, there's only one professional dungeon in the state with a fully operational medical exam room, set up to provide traction.

It had been almost more than our budget could bear.

I looked up at the monitor, which still showed me, spread, naked, used. Glistening with sweat, painted like a tramp. I watched as it showed my pussy, tits, face. I felt my clit swelling. My hand slowly slid down my belly, still marked by the angry red impressions of the brace.

I touched my pussy, feeling it wet, hot, and aching. I began to stroke my clit, feeling another orgasm surprise me as it began to pulse into being.

Expensive, yes. But oh, so worth it.

I heard the hospital bed groaning and squeaking in protest as I came.

Cocked and Loaded

Thomas S. Roche

I usually don't speed, but this time it can't be helped. You hug my body as I hug the curves, leaning low into the seat. You keep your hand above my waist only because I've made you promise to do so—to transgress would be dangerous. But I can tell, this time in particular, that it's an effort for you.

I merge the Triumph onto the freeway, hitting sixty, seventy, seventy-five, and you grip me with your spread thighs tight against my hips. The wind whistles past us. You've unzipped your jacket, and even through the back of mine, I can feel them. Firm, insistent, unforgiving. And it's not because of the cold.

I can still feel our positions reversed, your body in my arms, your back against my front, me leaning down to line my eyes up with yours, smelling the scent of your hair and feeling your pigtails brush against my shoulders. I can still feel your ass against mine, pressing against my crotch, your tight jeans smooth and your round butt wriggling maybe a little more than it needs to. I can still hear you say, "I can't," a little pathetic whimper designed, I suspect, to get me to do exactly what I'm doing: to curl my arms around you, put my hands on yours, and help you steady them. "You can," I tell you, and your body tenses as you pull the trigger.

The Magnum explodes in front of us, its four-inch barrel erupting in a flash of death, and you let out a yelp, a scream—and then a trembling giggle as I help you put down the gun, pointing downrange. You bring your hand to your mouth, gasping. A hole has appeared between the eyes of the shadowed target.

"I hit it," you say in a faint moan, as I put my arms around you and hug you. I realize, in an instant, that your nipples are so hard that they hurt my wrist as I brush by your breasts. Your ass is pushed back firmly against my crotch, my now hard cock resting centered in the furrow between your cheeks.

"Beginner's luck," I whisper, and you reach for the gun.

I can still feel it all as we pull into the driveway, stinking of cordite and flop sweat. Now I understand why you needed to fire a .44 Magnum for your first gun, why you begged me to leave the Glock at home, why you said you'd do anything if I'd keep the Sig .380 in the gun safe in the back of the closet. And I know why I agreed.

Because I remember, perhaps even more vividly than the first shot, how you glanced behind us, made sure the clerk wasn't watching through the filthy bulletproof glass; how you unfastened the top button of your incredibly low-slung jeans, took my cordite-stinking hand in yours, shoved it underneath.

No panties—I knew that, or I could have guessed it, because I've seen you in these jeans and I know even the skimpiest thong shows above your waistband. But tonight, for your virgin foray into squirting lead, you've got nothing at all under those tight low-rise jeans. Nothing but your pussy, smooth and shaved and—I find out as you force my finger into you—dripping. No, not dripping. Pouring. It's a wonder your jeans aren't soaked through. You ease my hand out of you, bring it to your face and lick my finger, breathing deeply, making love to the tip of my pussy-slick finger, inhaling its scent.

"Ever notice how pussy and gunpowder smell sort of the same?" you ask.

"Not until now," I say.

I understand it now—I understand a few things, maybe more than a few. Why, when you found out—after our first night together—that I was a cop, you searched all over the Net for interesting facts about women and guns, quoting them to me from obscure websites while I cleaned my service Beretta on the coffee table. Why you "happened" along schoolgirls-with-guns.com and giggled for hours with me over the ludicrously cheesy photos of scantily-clad pigtailed girls with assault rifles.

Why that was the night we fucked so hard we broke the bed, I was late to work, and you called me at my desk the next day to masturbate on the phone for me while I sat uncomfortably amid the hubbub of the squad room. Why you started begging me to take you to the shooting range, show you how to shoot—not just any old gun, but the .44 Magnum my father left me.

Why, when you showed up at my place for the ride to the

range, you were wearing those low-rise jeans with the flowers down the sides, a skintight Britney Spears crop top too obscene for its namesake to ever get away with on national television, and your hair in pigtails. The guys at the gun shop couldn't take their eyes off you, their gazes of abject lust thicker than the smoke in the room as their eyes roved over your erect nipples showing through the top—but then, nobody fucks with a well-armed schoolgirl.

I shove you against the wall the second we're in the house, holding you hard with my whole body. I set down the gun case and rip off your jacket, exposing your firm breasts through the crop top. Your nipples are so hard they feel like rocks against my chest, and it's not from the ride. You're not wearing a bra.

"Will you give it to me?" you whisper into my ear as I devour you, my mouth biting and sucking at your neck, your shoulders, your cleavage. "Will you give me what I want, Officer?"

I step back, my cock throbbing in my pants.

"What's that?" I ask you.

"Oh," you say. "I think you know."

Wriggling out from under me, you pick up the gun case and saunter into the combination living room/bedroom. You set the gun case down on the bed. I watch as you kick off your Adidas and slowly unzip your incredibly tight pants. You have to squirm and struggle to slide out of them; I can see as you bend all the way over to take them over your ankles that your pussy really is smooth, smooth as silk—and that your jeans really are soaked. You stand up partway and look over your shoulder at me, your pigtails framing your gorgeous face and your smooth, round asscheeks framing your bare pussy.

Slowly, you crawl onto the bed, stretching out. You've still got the crop top on, maybe because you like the sense of innocence it imparts. I don't doubt it. But however innocent Britney may be, your tits with their hard nipples spell out that you're anything but. You cuddle up with the gun case and unzip it.

"Be careful with that," I tell you, and you smile coquettishly, as if daring me to stop you.

I stand watching, my cock hard in my jeans, my motorcycle boots planted firmly—I couldn't stop you if I wanted to.

You take the .44 Magnum out. It takes me a moment to realize you've switched the gun case—it's not the one I take to the shooting range, now. It's the one I use when I'm playing with you. This isn't the gun I shoot; it's the one I use to fuck you. It's identical to the gun I shoot with in every way—from the outside. But it's a stage gun, one that wouldn't even shoot a starter round if they made them in .44. The cylinders are filled, and there's no firing pin on the hammer. The barrel is solid, despite the fact that its opening looks black and dangerous like that of a real gun. If I hadn't removed the bright-orange cap that the barrel came with—that cap the law requires to make sure the cops don't shoot some B-movie actress by accident, thinking she's got a real gun—it wouldn't look real at all. But I did, and it does.

You lick your way down the four-inch stainless steel barrel. Spreading your legs, you ease the gun between them and, holding the gun upside down, nuzzle the muzzle of the gun between the shaved lips of your sex.

"Don't you need some lube?" I ask.

You shake your head, *no*.

The barrel disappears into your pussy, and you moan "Oh, god, oh, god, oh, god." Usually when you're rubbing yourself to orgasm, you take it slow, warming up, getting yourself all hot. This time it's none of that—just slam, bam, thank you, Ma'am. You shove the gun as deep as it will go and rub yourself as fast as you can. You come almost instantly, twisting and writhing on the bed.

When you come to a stop, you look up at me flirtatiously and lick your lips.

I want to touch my cock so bad, to climb up and slide it into you. But I have to watch—like one of your strip club patrons getting a lap dance, I can watch, smell, hunger—but not touch.

You spread your legs wide and set the gun between them on the bed. Your hands resting on your thighs, you look right at me.

"What do you say, Officer? Will you give a little girl what she really wants?"

I'm on you in an instant, the Sig coming out of my belt pouch before you can gasp. You know I pack, twenty-four/seven—a sexy silver-finish Sig-Sauer .380 that you've always been fascinated with. But you never expected to have it shoved in your mouth. You never expected to suck it.

The fact that I've switched guns, too—grabbing my second stage gun, the automatic I like because its barrel is thicker and I can fuck you with both barrel and slide—hasn't escaped you. The Sig is just as safe as the .44, but you don't care. In our fantasy, it's a real gun—cocked and loaded.

My knee is between your legs, holding you down, as your

eyes go wide. You're sucking on the barrel like it was my cock.

Your eyes are wide and I see excitement in them like I've never seen. "You like it, baby? You like tasting danger? You want to play on the edge?"

I see the effect my threat has on you. The terror heightened, your nipples become even more evident through the shirt.

"Reach for the Magnum," I tell you. "Fuck yourself."

I look down at the glittering revolver, wondering who owns you.

You pick up the gun, turn the barrel toward your pussy, ease it up to your sex.

"Pull the hammer back."

I hear the hammer clicking back, feel your body shivering with terror. "Put it in," I tell you, my cock so hard I can hardly stand it.

This time your cunt is tight, tight from the anticipation. The gun won't go in at first.

"You asked for it. Now take it."

Finally the barrel slides into your cunt, and you can't stop the spasms of your body as your back arches and you shiver back. Now I'm on top of you, my hand between your legs, holding both guns and shoving the .44 deeper into you. I've got the Sig out of your mouth and against your head now, dripping with saliva. You're sobbing. Sobbing because you're about to come, and even in these short months we've been together I've learned to recognize the sighs. I work the .44 around so the barrel is hitting your G-spot, and that's when your mouth goes wide, drool leaking out and soaking the front of your T-shirt, making your tits even more evident. I feel you grabbing for my belt, ripping open my pants as I fuck you.

Both your hands wrap around my cock, and it only takes a few quick, expert strokes before I know I'm going to come.

You, too. Maybe it's the feel of my hot jizz mingling with the gun oil, or maybe it's the click of the .44 inside you as I pull the trigger, the hammer falling on filled-in cylinders. Either way, we both explode and I come so hard I feel liquid shooting onto my chest, look down as it soaks through your drool-spattered top. Crying, you writhe under me as I feel the .44 twitching with the spasms of your body.

Gently, I ease the gun out. I toss it on the pillow next to you.

The fact that neither gun is real didn't do anything to lessen our excitement. Because that's who you are, whether you're begging me to fuck you with a .44 Magnum or tempting all the rednecks down at the gun shop. You're dangerous—you're a living, breathing, flirting, dripping edge scene. Whether you're jerking me off onto your tits or cuddled up in my arms, fake guns strewn across the bed.

Cocked and loaded, baby, that's you.

Evening Class
J. Hadleigh Alex

The end of the office day draws near. He phones home. It rings three times.

She answers. "Is there anything you want to ask me?" Her voice is quiet, almost a whisper.

"Yes," he says. Her mouth is close to the phone. He listens to her breath—measured, deep, with a hint of a tremble. After a pause, he asks, "Have you done your homework?"

A sigh. "Most of it," she says.

"Make sure it's done by the time I'm home," he says, and hangs up. He's made the decision, now it's just a matter of time. Come five he takes his coat from the stand and puts it on, lifts his briefcase—already packed and shut—and, like a ghost, slips unnoticed from the office.

The house door clicks shut behind him. He drops his keys into the pocket of his coat as he hangs it up—one of many ritual reversals that punctuate the day.

The house is dark, though the welcoming aroma of a spicy supper wafts toward him, and soft, yellow light spills around the study door. He takes five steps toward it, pushing the door wide in front of him as he enters.

She's sitting at the desk, head bowed over an open book, but she looks up as he fills the doorway. She makes to rise, but he waves his hand in a circle to tell her to stay seated. He walks to her desk, stands to one side, peers at what she's reading.

Her long hair, straight and black, tumbles onto the pages, and he can't read the words. He places one hand on her shoulder and eases her back from the studious hunch she's adopted. As he does so, his gaze takes in the view down the front of her blouse—her generous bosom revealed in the deep V-shape of her unbuttoned collar. No tie this evening; is that mere fashionable variation, or rebellion? No matter, this he will decide later.

He takes her chin in his hand, lifting her face up so that he can see her eyes. Her soft skin is warm against his fingertips. He repeats his earlier question.

"Have you done your homework?"

She blinks, and he feels the rippling tension in her neck as she swallows. "Most of it," she says, in an echo of her previous response.

"That's what you said when last I asked you," he says. "Have you done no more?"

She blinks again, and makes to shake her head, but still he grips her chin, and he feels rather than sees the movement.

"My dear," he says, letting her face fall. "You know that isn't good enough."

She nods, and her black tresses brush the book once more, like curtains at an open window. She doesn't look at him, but stares at the floor.

"You know, as well…" he continues, walking over to the clear expanse of his rosewood bureau, "…what this means, don't you?" He opens a drawer.

Her hands grip each side of her desk as she stands up. "Yes, sir. I do."

He hears the catch in her throat.

He looks at her. The writing surface hides her legs, but not the gray, pleated skirt curving around the contours of her hips. It's short enough to reveal a flash of thigh above the desk's varnished, ink-stained wood.

"Come here, girl." He points to his bureau, immaculate and clear, an embossed leather inlay its only decoration.

She sighs, shuffles sideways from her desk and walks slowly toward him. Her legs are bare. No stockings, not even white ankle-socks, hide the lissome sweep of her calves, or the subtle promise of her thighs soaring up behind the hem of her skirt. On her feet, patent-leather high heels accentuate the wily provocation of her walk.

He shakes his head. Will she never learn? How much discipline do such lessons take? He *tut-tuts* to himself and moves his hand above the bureau. "You know the procedure," he says.

She looks at him across the vast leather and rosewood expanse, then her gaze drops to its surface. She nods. She places her hands on the dark, polished wood, then leans forward, letting her palms slide toward him as she lowers her body to the bureau. When her hands have almost reached his side of it, he grasps her wrists and pulls them toward him; she lets out a gasp as he yanks them so that she can grip the edge of the desk. The tails of her blouse pull free of her skirt's waistband, revealing the pale skin of her lower back.

Now that she's stretched out across the leather, he reaches into the bureau drawer and removes a transparent plastic ruler. He brings it down with a crack, just millimeters from her face, and she flinches at its resounding proximity.

"Homework not done. Not wearing a tie. Nonregulation shoes." With each recitation of her misdemeanors he slaps the ruler down. "You know that means extra punishment." Her head twitches with the slightest nod.

He walks round to her side of the bureau and stands behind her. She's bent across the surface but her legs are straight, the gray fabric of her skirt barely covering her rear.

With finger and thumb he takes the hem of her skirt and pulls it up, high above her waist, revealing her backside. An involuntary whistle escapes his lips at the sight: this timid girl is wearing a sheer, lace thong. The pastel pink fabric, tailored to a tiny triangle below the small of her back, disappears between her cheeks, the twin globes of her bare buttocks presenting a perfect target for her imminent chastisement.

"Not a word, now," he says, letting the wide plastic blade oscillate in the air as he takes aim. And then he strikes; the ruler swishes down, catching her exposed cheeks full and flat with a satisfying smack, sending ripples radiating down her thighs.

"Ow!" Her cry is gasped out, then stifled almost before it's audible.

"Silence!" He bends close to her head and speaks into her ear. "You know the rules." Only strokes received without a murmur will count toward her punishment. Her transgressions this evening have already mounted up; she can ill afford to add to her tally.

The second stroke is harder than the first, but precisely registered, and though she takes it without crying out he can tell it's an effort. Her body shudders in response to the blow, and she screws her eyes shut. The third and fourth strokes follow in quick succession, and each time she convulses her reaction, but in silence. Her cheeks are now beginning to respond, lighting the ruler's path in ruby neon.

The fifth blow he delivers from a greater height; she hears the hiss of air as it descends, and tenses up, clenching her cheeks in anticipation. But this serves only to harden the ruler's target, the plastic making firmer contact, sharpening the pain.

She's breathing heavily now, and despite the movements of her bottom as she squirms her body in acute discomfort, he lands the sixth stroke with confirmed accuracy, bringing her protesting cheeks to a rosy glow. Her scorched backside radiates a satisfying heat into his palm as he holds it close, testing his handiwork.

"Good girl," he says, and she relaxes into the surface of the bureau. "But now we must take account of certain facts." He sees her body jerk with renewed tension as she realizes her punishment isn't over. "This underwear," he says, tracing his finger along the edge of the lacy fabric where it plunges between her cheeks, "is entirely out of order, and must be removed."

He stands behind her bent body and tucks the fingers of both hands behind the waistband of the thong; he crouches, pulling the thong downward, letting the narrow string slip over her reddened flesh. The string pulls out from its snug captivity deep between her buttocks, the waistband rolling itself into a thin cord as it travels down to her ankles.

He stands, and takes the waist of her pleated skirt in one hand, and with the other unzips it at the side and pulls it away. He pauses for a moment over the sight of her naked rear, then walks once more to his side of the bureau, where her hands still grip the edge, stretching her body across the leather.

"It's time we saw precisely what we're at," he says, leaning forward to reach over her head and grasp the tails of her blouse. With a fluid motion he pulls the white cotton up her back toward her shoulders, and the front of it rides up between her chest and the bureau's leather inlay. His insistent pull causes the garment to catch on her breasts as they press into the leather, but he continues the rough divestment until the fabric has gone over her head and traveled to her wrists. On his guidance she releases her grip, hand by hand, and he peels the blouse away.

She now stretches naked across the leather, her hair pulled up by the removal of the blouse, revealing a pale-skinned back narrowing to a slim waist, and hips that broaden to a pair of luscious, rounded buttocks streaked in angry red.

For the second time he reaches into the drawer, and removes a long, narrow cane. In his hand it feels light, but sharp, as he whips it around above the girl's prone form. She moans at its hissing passage through the air. This won't be the first time her skin has felt the sharp crack of the cane, and her body tenses at the memory, anticipating its relentless scourge.

He takes aim, eyeing up his target—her reddening cheeks

drawing his gaze to the epicenter of her shapely form. He raises his hand high, pauses for accuracy, and with one quick swish brings the cane down in a precise slash, to land squarely on one buttock. The resounding smack echoes through the room as the painful jolt radiates from the point of contact, rippling across her skin—the natural vibration combining with an involuntary muscle spasm.

He can see the pain. She strains to keep it within her, screwing her eyes shut, as if opening them would let the sensation stream out of her in agony. But while she holds it in, he wastes no time and brings the cane down on the other cheek, making a harsh red line to mirror the first. Once more she shudders her resistance in agonized silence, letting a rush of breath escape her open mouth.

He looks her over, sees the sheen of sweat on her skin and the droplets forming on her spine, running together, gathering in a tiny pool in the small of her back. On the bureau, the leather is moist where her perspiring skin moves against it.

He returns his attention to her crisscrossed backside, and readies himself for his next strokes. The cane is a precise instrument, its surface texture just right for its purpose. He must judge the force to use on her—a swinging blow, as powerful as possible, without actually breaking the skin. This is what he gives her, landing a precise inch away from the cane's first strike. She jolts in agony once more, and he knows she can hardly bear it. But the regularity of her punishment cannot be interrupted. She must lie there, willing to receive the just rewards for her transgressions.

The air above her snaps in two as he brings the cane down again, completing the second pair of stripes. Once more he surveys the damage. Her red cheeks stand out in contrast to the sober study decor, and the pale flesh of her back and legs quiver in time with her snatched, shallow breathing. It's clear that she's reacting to the severity of her chastisement, and that she's only a couple of strokes away from completing penance for her sins.

And so he administers the first of the final strokes, swishing the cane down from high above his head, to land perpendicular across the first two strokes on one buttock.

She convulses as it hits. The bite of the cane is precise, raising a further welt across her cheek, with a bright spot at each of the stroke's intersections with its two predecessors.

The final stroke sends an equal spasm through her as it bites into the other cheek, finalizing the scarlet symmetry.

She's done. She's paid her price. Her backside's patterned lines bear witness to her ordeal. He lays the cane down on the bureau, and gently places his palms on those neon-striped globes. The heat from them is unbelievable. He squeezes the soft flesh, allowing his thumbs to slide into the welcoming crevice between her cheeks.

He spreads her. She moans as he exposes the hidden recesses within, pressing one hand deep into her. His fingers find her moist, and swollen. He removes his hand, lifts it to his face, smelling her heavy scent. It's time. She's ready.

He steps back from the welted redness of her tortured butt and quickly undresses, and in a moment he has his heavy, expectant organ pressing between her buttocks' soft flesh. He can feel her heat on him. He leans into her, grasping her waist in his hands, gripping her yielding body. His hands slide up between the bureau's sweat-smeared leather and her hot skin, and her breasts succumb to his caresses, her nipples hard between his fingers and thumbs.

His erection continues to jut into her, straining to find its way. With care he leans back, sliding his hands down over her back, to rest for a moment on her radiant buttocks, then to slip between them, spreading those fulsome globes.

Her flesh is parted. She's exposed, revealing her slick pink slit, and he maneuvers his hardened shaft toward its target. He pauses at her entrance, relishing the expectation of her secret grip on his purpled engorgement. And then he pushes home, sliding the bold rod of flesh into her, feeling her heat, her pressure, her muscular containment as she takes him within her.

She's hot, and wet. His progress, though unimpeded, is resisted just enough to bring him to a delicious height of sensual pleasure as he plunges and withdraws in measured strokes.

He keeps his rhythm, but he can feel her tension as she comes before he does, her muscles alternately gripping and releasing him, her slick wetness growing to a flood around his member. But still he pumps her, maintaining his unhurried oscillations, drinking in the pleasure of her responsive flesh engulfing his.

She's gasping now and letting out unintelligible squeaks as he continues his measured thrusts. Her gasps grow deeper, her squeaking grows to pronounced cries, and all the while he's getting closer to his own fulfillment. Her orchestrated arousal tells him she's near, and so he concentrates, slowing his thrusts, feeling her body tense and relax, aware of his own impending climax as the fire of his orgasm travels up the shaft of his organ to the pressured head, its stretched skin so sensitive to every nuance of her engulfing flesh, until, as the well of his climax rises, his member throbbing inside her, he grips her body and comes in a flood of pulsating pleasure. As his tidal wave breaks within her, it is enough, the final sensation, to send her over the edge into ecstasy, and she convulses, letting out a lasting, helpless sigh.

The end of the office day draws near. He phones home. It rings three times.

She answers. "Is there anything you want to ask me?" Her voice is quiet, almost a whisper.

"Yes," he says.

Dinner Out

MARIE SUDAC

I've been hurting for it so long that the smell of you hits me as soon as I enter the house, and I feel my body respond with the kind of hunger I've been nursing with melancholy sadness for a whole week. I unbutton my blazer in the kitchen, kick off my pumps in the living room, strip off my blouse and my skirt in the hall. By the time I nudge open the door of the bedroom and see you in bed, sprawled out sweaty and naked in the tangled sheets, my pussy is already aching. The moist sheets splay across your belly, and your skin glistens in the slanted light from the window. You're asleep, snoring lightly. I don't even take off my garter belt and stockings before I climb into bed with you. And I don't even kiss you hello before I press my body against yours and cradle your cock, half-hard as you sleep.

Your eyes pop open and I shiver as you look at me with naked lust. Your cock hardens quickly in my hand, and my pussy responds with such a hot flood of juice that before I know I'm

MARIE SUDAC

doing it, I've burrowed under the covers and taken your cock in my mouth. The taste of it fills me with a rush of sensation, and my nipples harden painfully in my too-tight bra. I want to take it off, but I find I can't do anything except wrap my fingers around the base of your cock and push you deeper into my mouth until I feel your swelling head against the entrance to my throat. When I reach down to my panties, it's to slide my fingers into them and feel my wetness, coating my fingers so I can reach back up and push them into your mouth. You bite my fingertips, hard, then lick my fingers clean and seize my hand to bite the heel of it while I suck you. I whimper softly, my noises muffled by the fullness of your cock in my throat as I bob up and down on you. I wore a thong today, thinking of you. It hurts me to take your cock out of my mouth, and my slick lips draw a glistening string of drool and pre-come from your cockhead as I sit up and straddle you, plucking the tiny crotch of my thong out of the way so I can sit down on your cock.

Your hands cradle my hips as I push onto you, my pussy so wet that it engulfs your cock in one hot, easy motion. In an instant I feel the familiar push of your cockhead against my G-spot, and I moan as I start to stroke my clit. I look down into your eyes and love you more than ever, wanting you to come inside me, wanting to come hard on your cock. And I'm close—very, very close.

Your hips rise up to meet me and I pump mine rhythmically; I feel my orgasm approaching. I'm on the very edge of it when you roll me off of you and tumble me onto the bed, face up, under you, legs spread. The feel of your weight almost makes me come right then, but you slide out of me and hold your cock erect, an inch from my cunt.

Moaning, whimpering, desperate, I inch my hips up and try to push myself back onto you. You tease me, pulling back. When I thrust myself hard at you, hungrily seeking your cock, you look down into my eyes and laugh.

You shake your head.

"Not yet," you say. "Get dressed. I'm taking you out to dinner."

"Baby, I'm so close," I whimper.

You smile broadly, climbing out of bed. "I want you aching for it. Get dressed."

I stretch out, sliding my hands into my wet thong and rubbing my clit. "Please?" I whisper.

"No," you say, getting back on the bed and grasping my wrists. You kiss me tenderly on the lips, your tongue stroking mine. That only makes me want it more, and I struggle against you, trying to get my hands back between my legs. I rub against you, feeling your wet cock on my belly.

"Come for me, then? Come on me?" I beg you. "Come in my mouth," I whisper.

You shake your head. "Get dressed in something nice—something very nice. This is an excellent restaurant. Be sure to wear gloves, though. Satin ones. And don't change your underwear—I love what you're wearing."

I should know better than to argue with you when you want to play these games. I love them as much as you do; for every whine and whimper I give you, begging you to come, to let me come, I know I'll come ten times harder when you finally let me have it.

But now, after a week without you, I want it so bad I can't control myself. I put my arms around you as you button your dress shirt; I drop to my knees and take your cock in my mouth again, tasting my pussy's juices so sharp on your hard flesh. You let me suck you, kneeling in my bra and panties. You let me take you into my throat, rub you all over my face. You let me bring you almost to the point where you'll come in my mouth; I taste the first tiny squirt of pre-come, and the flavor overwhelms me, making me want you more than I've ever wanted you in my life. I swallow eagerly and suck you harder, waiting for your come.

But you pull back, holding my hair, forcing my head back so that my lips and tongue work, empty and aching, an inch from your cock. I look up at you and whimper, then hear myself moaning, "Please? Please? Please?"

But you shake your head, pull me to my feet, and point me at the closet. It hurts to walk, my clit is so swollen. My hands quiver as I select my sexiest minidress, a tight little black number. I need your help zipping it, and the feel of your fingers on my skin makes me bite my lip. I put on a string of pearls, a dose of mascara, a thick coat of bright red lipstick. You knot a red tie around your neck and put on your dark wool suit coat.

I wear high-heeled shoes, praying you'll fuck me in them, like you did the last time we played this game. Only this time, something in your eyes tells me that the ante has been upped more than even I can imagine.

I don't bother with my seat belt in the car; it's much more important to me to tuck my ankles under my ass and cuddle up against your warm body as you drive.

I ask you how your trip was; I wonder out loud, again, why you chose to drive from Vancouver rather than flying, especially since your work would have paid for it. "I wanted to pick something up in Oregon," you tell me mysteriously. When I ask you what it is, you tell me I'll find out soon enough. That makes my pussy feel swollen and wet. I'm so turned on I'm still leaking, thick pulses of juice oozing out of my cunt and soaking my thong until it's so wet it feels cold and clammy. But when I push my thighs together tightly, it soon warms up.

We drive into the city and into the financial district. As the sun goes down, you go slowly along the less savory streets, like you're looking for a hooker. I think for a moment that maybe you are—maybe that's what you've got in store for me, why you wanted me so aching and wet that I couldn't say no. Are you going to push me to my knees in front of a twenty-five-dollar whore in a cheap red minidress, knowing I can't deny you anything, knowing I'll slip my tongue into her cunt just to get you to fuck me till I come? Knowing I'm yours, no matter what you do to me?

I think I have my answer when you pull into an alley, a dark one leading behind the newspaper loading dock and the back end of an office building. By now it's completely dark, and the alley stretches into blackness with not a streetlight anywhere to be seen. You hit the button that unlocks my door.

"Walk to the far end," you tell me.

"Honey, what…?"

You lean over and kiss me. "No questions," you say. "Just do it."

Nervously, I get out, taking my purse. You reach over and snatch it away from me, smiling.

"You won't need this," you say. "Walk quickly and with determination."

As I start walking, I hear you putting the car in reverse. I listen to the scratch of your tires as you pull back into traffic and disappear. Now I'm lost in the blackness of the alley, shaking with my fear. I try to walk quickly, but it's hard in these high heels. Each time I pass one of the empty cul-de-sacs that sports sleeping street people, I catch their harsh scent and try to hold my breath. But there's no clean air to be drawn. Each time I pass a tiny side alley, I feel the thumping heartbeat of terror that someone is waiting there for me, waiting to hurt me. I feel the familiar bite of tears in my chest, the quiver of my throat as it closes from mounting terror.

I walk as quickly as I can, listening to the echoing click of my high heels. The fear is making the ache in my pussy feel dangerous. It's making my knees feel weak. It's making my nipples hard, harder than they ever could have gotten from arousal alone. None of this feels good, however; it's all sheer terror; sheer pain; sheer hateful, forced surrender. I feel my eyes moisten and I choke back a single sob, then a second, then a third. I walk faster. Past another open, blackened alley.

I'm trying to watch for it. I'm trying to be aware, awake, alert, observant, but my tears have blinded my eyes, rendering me helpless—paralyzing me. The arm comes out from blackness and seizes my hair, jerking me back against a hard, unfamiliar body. For an instant I pray it's you, and then I smell the filth and the ancient, soured sweat. I open my mouth to scream. The arm closes around my throat, and I see the hand in front of me in the shadows, black-gloved. I hear the click and a glistening stream of silver erupts in the darkness, reflecting a single band of light from high, high above. Then the arm pulls me back into darkness, and all I can do is feel the blade against my throat.

"Don't scream," I hear the raspy voice. "Or you're finished."

Now I know why you drove through Oregon; switchblades are legal there. You push me forward across a cold metal garbage can, bending me over as you seize my hair. The tears grab me and I hear myself sobbing even as my pussy floods to feel you pushing hard against me from behind. I can feel your cock in your pants and it terrifies me even as it makes my clit throb. You grasp my hair tightly and I feel the cold steel of your blade sliding between my dress and my skin.

It's not even a ripping sound. The blade is so sharp it barely makes any noise at all. The only way I know you've cut my dress from back to hem is when it falls off of me. You slice each strap neatly, holding my hair so tight I can't do anything but squirm and sob. My dress is in shreds, and I feel the cold night air against my flesh. You cut each strap of my bra and it, too, falls in ruined pieces. Then my garter belt, garters first, low, close to the clasps, then waistband. My stockings fall. You pull me up, hard, by my hair, so that I'm standing there, almost naked. All I have on now are satin gloves, a string of pearls, and my thong and stockings. The stockings have already slid down to my knees, weighted by the garter clasps. You reach out and stab the remains of my dress with your knife, flick the ruined garment into a puddle of urine. With it goes my bra, or what's left of it, and my garter belt is already tattered at my feet. My arms hang helpless at my sides, shaking, as you caress my throat with the tip of a switchblade I now know is sharp enough to cut silk and satin without ripping.

Your breath is hot against my ear as you twist your hand in my hair. I can smell your filth, the rough wool overcoat you wear soaked in old sweat and god knows what else. But it's open in front, so I can feel your cock pressing hard through your suit pants, long and threatening between my cheeks. Hard and ready to fuck me. Ready to rape me.

You jerk my head, pulling my hair so firmly I have to choke back another sob, fight the urge to scream. Some part of me thinks you really might slit my throat. Some part of me thinks you're really going to rape me.

You draw the knife tip down between my breasts, taking a moment to tease my nipples. The fear has hardened them until they hurt enough to make me cry on their own. But the tip of your knife makes them ache in a different way, flushing shame and humiliation through my body, making my chest hot as my full breasts quiver with my sobs.

You finish with my breasts, draw the knife down over my soft belly, pressing just hard enough to let me know that, pressing any harder, you would gut me. My arms hang limp, my entire body helpless in your grasp.

You slip the edge of the blade under the front of my panties. I think you're going to cut them off. Instead, you twist my hair harder, so hard I gasp.

Then you bring the knife slowly back up my belly, circling each of my nipples and letting it come to rest at my throat, where it scares me the most.

"Take them off," you tell me.

I shake. I don't move. I stand there frozen under your terrible assault, knowing the word I should say to stop this, the word that will let you know you've gone too far. I look into the shadows and think I see distant shapes—men watching. Waiting their turn.

You press very gently against my throat, making me feel the prick of it.

The word is on my lips, in my tongue, but my lips are too tight and my tongue is too swollen with excitement and fear. I can feel my cunt throbbing with each beat of my pulse against the tip of your knife.

You shake my head with your hand tight in my hair, and I would swear I could feel the trickle of blood down the front of my throat. You growl in a voice I've never heard from you:

"Take them down," you say. "Pull your fucking panties down, bitch."

Whimpering, terrified, I force my useless hands to move, reaching to the thin string of my thong panties and pulling them down over my hips, over my ass. Peeling the crotch off of my pussy, feeling how it's so wet it sticks. Feeling how the bare flesh tingles with the freezing night air.

"All the way," you order me, and I tug my panties down to my thighs, having to stretch since you won't let go of my hair. Since you won't let me move at all, won't let me bend over.

I let go, and my panties slide down my thighs to my knees and then stop. They're so tight they lodge between my knees. You shake your fist again, jiggling my whole body against your knife. My panties drop down over my shins and bunch around my ankles.

"Step out of them," you tell me.

I do, my legs quaking. It's so much more humiliating, being forced to take my own panties off, being forced to reveal myself to you. But you've got more humiliating things in store for me, as you pull me hard against you and tell me:

"Spread your legs."

Nervously, I open them, moving very slowly so you don't cut me. I have to bend forward to spread them, but as I do you shove me hard, and in that instant you must have slipped the blade away, because I don't find myself impaled on it. Instead, I'm sprawled over the garbage can lid, legs spread, arms thrust out desperately, body shaking.

"Wider, bitch," you say.

I obey this time, shocked and terrified by the sudden burst of force. I spread my legs as wide as I can, so wide I feel my feet pushing into the mounds of garbage off to the side. So wide I feel myself helpless, off balance, opened up to you.

I realize with horror, with excitement, that it's time. You're going to rape me.

You don't go slow; you don't tease me. Your cock drives into me so fast that if I wasn't already gushing wet, it would make me scream in pain. I scream anyway, in shock and fear, even as the thickness of your cock explodes through me and makes every muscle in my body strain with sudden pleasure. You grab my hair and lean forward hard, bearing me into the garbage can as you drive your cock violently into me. I feel the prick of the knife against my throat and you growl, "Scream again and you're dead, bitch!" But my mouth is already open wide, and it's all I can do to turn that scream into a long, low moan as I feel your cock pounding into me. You've shoved me forward so roughly that my pubic bone is pressed against the rim of the garbage can, forcing pressure hard against my clit. I'm close to coming already, and the sobs have turned to gasps and moans of pleasure. But before I can come, you pull out of me and snarl, "You're so wet your pussy's loose, bitch. Let's see how you like it back here," and before I know what's happening my cheeks are spread around the thickness of your thumb, forcing me wide open. My eyes go wide and I start to gasp, "No, no—!" The safeword springs to my lips but never makes it out. Your thumb slides out, replaced by your cock as you shove into me so hard that it feels like you should rip me in two—but you don't; my wet pussy is still dripping from your cock, and it forces its way into me with violence matched only by the pleasure it drives through my naked body. I open my mouth wider than ever, so wide I feel my jaw popping, the corners of my mouth stretched painfully, and as your cock sinks into my ass I push back onto you, fucking myself onto it. Your hand comes around and you seize my hair to keep me from moving, and I feel the coldness of the knife sliding up my thigh. I would scream, then, as I feel the sharp tip of it pushing between my lips, but there isn't even time for me to scream—because I'm right on the edge of coming. As you shove the knife into me, your cock filling my ass, your violent pounding ripping me every bit as much as a knife blade ever could, I let out an uncontrolled, desperate scream of orgasm, terror mingling with pleasure and heightening every sensation coursing through my naked body. Sobs wrack me as you drive it handle-deep into me, and I feel its cold, hard hilt pushed up against my tender opening even as it spasms with orgasm. You pound into me, another thrust, another, and then you let out a scream of your own as you shoot deep into my ass. I lie there bent over the garbage can, naked, helpless, terrified, not sure whether I'm alive or dead. You pull your spent cock out of my ass and a stream of your come oozes down my inner thigh. You're gone in an instant, and I hear your footsteps echoing as you vanish down the dark alley.

I don't know how long I lie there over the garbage can, naked, spread, ass and cunt fucked wide. Just long enough for me to come to my senses, pull myself off the garbage can, and cross my satin-shrouded arms over my naked breasts, shivering.

As I stand there in the garbage-strewn darkness, I reach down and touch my pussy. It's wide, dripping, and it aches with every touch. My clit throbs, still hard, wanting more though hurting from the rough press of the metal garbage can. But my cunt is intact, neither cut nor bleeding.

My clothes, however, are nothing more than shredded rags all around me.

I stand there exposed, frightened, feeling off balance in my high-heeled shoes and the stockings bunched around my ankles, feeling the warm brush of my satin gloves against my breasts as I struggle to hide them—from whom, I don't know. Pearls dangle between my breasts, looking odd and ridiculous.

The alley explodes in a blaze of light, and I turn, stunned, looking into the headlights. The police? A stranger?

You get out of the car, throw your suit jacket over me, and lead me otherwise naked into the car. You close the passenger side door, get in.

I curl up against you, clutching you for support. I can feel the bulge of your pocket—two bulges, actually, and I know that it wasn't your knife I was so sure was cutting me deep when you slid it into my pussy. I press my palm against the dual handles of your weapons—one metal, to scare me, one rubber, to fuck me with. How could I have been so convinced you would really put a knife inside me? It doesn't matter. In the moment you slid it into me, I was yours, totally owned by your brutal persona, and that's why I came so hard. The part of you that took me so violently really *would* fuck me with a knife, and that's why I came so hard. But the more important part of you that loves me and cherishes me made sure that evil bastard was holding a knife that wouldn't do anything except what you wanted it do—to make me come, harder than I've ever come before.

I know you'd never hurt me—now, I know that. A moment ago I was sure you would, and that's why I love *you* more than anything. You went there with me, into a place that terrified us both. But now we're back in our real life, where you take care of me. You gently push me off of you, force my limp body into the seat, pull my seat belt over me and buckle it.

"Seat belts save lives," you tell me, and put the car in gear.

By the time we get home I'm half asleep, floating on a delicious cloud of fear and sex and hunger. You pull into the garage so the neighbors won't see me get out of the car nude except for your jacket. You lead me into the house, put me to bed, and bring me a tray of food—cold cuts and sourdough bread.

"It's not from a nice restaurant," you say. "But I hope it's okay for dinner."

I swallow a bite of bread and lean over to kiss you.

"I had my dinner," I whisper hoarsely. "It was delicious."

Pearl Necklace

JOLIE JOSS

We're just finishing up Sunday brunch at the Uptown Plaza when I get the text. As Rick goes on talking, I fish my smartphone out of my purse. My heart pounds as I read it. I go tingly all over. I feel like my temperature has just shot up about ten degrees.

I knew it was a possibility, but I didn't think it would really happen. I've been flirting with him online for months—three of them, and five days, to be exact. I didn't think he'd actually take me up on my offer of "Anytime, anyplace."

But now that he has, how can I say no?

"Rick, darling," I break in when he gives me half a chance. "I know we talked about spending the day together, but I'm afraid something's come up. I've got to show a property near here for work, all right? You understand, don't you? We can spend time together later."

At first Rick looks crestfallen, then suspicious. When my

wicked look confirms his worst suspicions, he looks confused, dismayed, and about to faint.

"I'll need the car," I tell him. "Be a dear and take a cab home. You've got cab fare, don't you?"

"Well, I—uh—" he sputters, not believing what he's hearing. "Yes, of course. It's just that…" He draws away and looks guilty.

"What, darling?"

"I bought you an anniversary present." He slips the small box out of his pocket and holds it out to me.

I open the package and smile.

"How nice, darling. A pearl necklace. Is that a hint?"

Rick gets flustered.

I wink at him. I stand and let him lift my cascade of red hair and clasp the necklace on me. I break out my compact, purse my lips, and admire myself wearing Rick's pearl necklace—knowing within just a few minutes I'll be wearing someone else's.

"It's so lovely, darling. I'm touched. Now, run along home. I'll be home when I'm finished." I run my hands along his neck and whisper: "Don't get too worked up on those downloads you like to watch. Save some for me, darling. Will you?"

Rick looks down and scampers away to the cab stand.

Just for the sake of appearances, I get out my parking receipt and stand lackadaisically in line. But lucky for me, the line at the parking window is longer than the line for a cab, so just as I reach the front, I see Rick disappear into the back of a Yellow, and I peel off for the elevator—leaving a briefly bewildered clerk.

I glance back, once, and spot Rick's eyes glaring from the

back of his taxi. Whether he spots me looking back at him, I won't know until after it's occurred, this thing I'm doing.

My *betrayal*.

And once that's done…everything will be different.

Online, I've cheated on him before. In chatrooms, I've gotten pearl necklaces from dozens of men not my husband. In phone calls, I've been unfaithful more times than I can count.

But not like this. Not in reality. And I never dreamed I could really do it so blatantly, ditching him after a perfectly lovely brunch. Not so carelessly, discarding my husband like a piece of used tissue and moving on to the next shiny cock. Not even caring that he suspects. Not even caring that he knows.

Not even caring that my husband's pearl necklace will soon be sticky with another man's come.

Or, on the contrary—being *turned on by it*. The very fact of my betrayal makes me wet. The very knowledge that he knows gets me so unbelievably aroused I can't control myself.

The looks of suspicion and confusion on my husband's face making me want to betray him so bad that I can't *not* cheat on him.

Like he's *begging for it*.

I open my phone again. The original text from Dion burns there on my screen: Room 1916. Behind it, a new text blinks.

It's a photo: Dion's cock. Big and thick and glorious, glistening even in this low-resolution photo. What is it about men? They think the cellular phone exists solely to send pictures of engorged genitals back and forth between cheating lovers. And perhaps more importantly, every man seems to think a JPEG of his cock makes a woman weak at the knees.

Well, when you meet men online, I suppose there's not much more they have to work with. And in this case, it was the very blatant nature of Dion's aggressive stance that made me cream. Wasn't that what I'd liked in all those hours of trading chat messages while I sat casually "working on some property spreadsheets" as Rick and I watched TV, my body turned "just so" to make sure Rick couldn't glimpse images of Dion's chest, abs, and cock?

Didn't I *beg* Dion to "grab me," "bend me over," "spank me," "pull my hair," "make me your slut"? Didn't I make him promise over and over again that if—no, not if, *when*—we met in person, he'd do all that and more? "Whenever, wherever?"

Didn't I beg him to push my boundaries?

And didn't I just "happen" to drop him a text to mention that Rick and I were planning on a nice leisurely Sunday, with brunch at the Uptown Plaza—which sometimes had very reasonable last-minute Sunday rates, and let you check in at noon if you asked nicely?

I'd done all of those things, hoping and praying that it would lead right where it was leading.

I'm sure as hell not backing out now.

I punch in a number and forwarded the JPEG, with a happy face.

Dion's left the door ajar. The comforter's folded on the floor. Ample light filters through the white gauze curtains to bathe the room in a gloriously flattering light, so when he's first revealed to me he looks about as good as a man can look.

Dion's stretched out nude and gorgeous across the hotel sheets, his dark skin accented by the bleached, starched white cotton. I see that he hasn't exaggerated a thing during our exten-sive online chats. Twenty-six—a full ten years younger than me—he's ripped and cut, with bulky forearms, big shoulders, and a broad chest. And his cock? Well...more on that later. His voice is just as delicious as it'd been all those long, late dirty talks while Rick was asleep, or pretending to be asleep.

"Hi," says Dion.

"Hello there, beautiful," I sigh.

I put out the DO NOT DISTURB sign and closed the door behind me.

There's no need to introduce ourselves. There's no need for the preliminaries usually engaged in by lovers meeting for the first time. He knows who I am. He knows me as intimately from my pictures as I know him from his. He knows far more of me, in fact, than he's seeing now, which is why it's so strange that my hands tremble as I start to undress for him. It always scares me to get naked in front of a man I've never fucked before, no matter how many dirty snapshots of me the guy's seen.

"Don't do that," he says. "Come over here. Let me."

I come to bed. Dion grabs me and pulls me onto him. I drop my purse beside the bed. Before I know it, he's got me pinned under his big, broad, muscular body. I melt into his scent and his heat and the feel of moisture against my skin. He's wet from the shower.

He kisses me, hard. His tongue is insistent. I react instantly to that first touch, and every further touch forces me deeper into his spell. But I'm still scared. In fact, I'm terrified.

I feel the need to talk or something. I feel the need to tell him how nervous I am to be cheating on Rick.

But when I try to pull away, he kisses me harder. He pins

me down. He holds my hair. He pulls my hair. His kisses plunge deeper. He violates me with his tongue. When I struggle a little bit more, he turns me over, pins me with his weight, and lifts his big hand up high.

"No talking," he says. "Not till I've fucked you."

Then he spanks me, just once, to still me. To *gentle* me. I'm his skittish little mare, and this is how he harnesses me.

It makes me warm all over. It makes my cunt wet.

"Yes, Sir," I say, and spread my legs.

He grabs my hips and lifts them high, forcing my ass into the air. He doesn't take my panties down. He doesn't take my skirt off. He just pulls the skirt up, the panties to the side, and exposes my Sunday-shaved cunt.

Then he fucks me from behind.

Just like that, I'm not a wannabe-adulteress anymore. I'm a real adulteress. Before I even know he's doing me, I'm done. I'm being fucked. He's in me, and I'm cheating.

There's no talk of a condom. All those discussions have been had. All those boundaries have been laid out. He goes into me bareback, his big stranger's cock naked, terrifying, and *hot*.

My cunt goes tight around him as he penetrates me. He's hard to take in this position, but I've been working on it. Yoga. Pilates. Deep knee bends. It's been the way I dreamt of Dion taking me since the beginning. "Something about your cock," I told Dion once during a filthy chat, once he showed me his dick. "It makes me want to get fucked in *this* position," and I sent him a JPEG mined from Rick's extensive porn collection, of a woman taking cock exactly like this. Face down. Ass up. Skirt lifted. Panties yanked to the side. Fully dressed, but fully exposed.

His huge cock stretches me. I'm so wet that I seem to

pour juice down over his cock as he slides in, but he still has to shove hard to penetrate me. He fits me like a glove and starts fucking me slowly, holding the crotch of my thin silky panties out of the way. My hands are flat against the hotel bed, my face pushed into the indentation left by Dion's body. I take him eagerly, ass in the air. I inhale his smell.

My body's a mass of sexual energy. I've been anticipating this for months, ever since the first time I laid eyes on Dion's photo. I've been dreaming of the moment when I would submit to his cock. But he is heavy on top of me, and all I can do is lay there and get fucked. It feels incredible, but I know there's no way I'm going to come. And I don't want to. All I want is to feel every inch of Dion's cock sliding into me over and over again, thrust after thrust, while he licks his thumb and works it up to my butthole.

He goes slowly at first, taking his time, stretching me out without ever quite entering me.

Then he takes me, with one thrust. I gasp as he inserts his thumb. He starts fucking my cunt deeper with his cock, holding his thumb as deep in my ass as he can as my muscles tighten around it. He thrusts his dick all the way into me. Feeling him inside both my holes five minutes after we've first kissed, I realize how deep I've gone into this. I've given myself to a total stranger. He's going to take me how he wishes.

That's when I realize he plans to make me come.

I never asked him if he was right or left handed. It's just not the sort of thing that occurs to one online. I realize now that he's right-handed, obviously, which is why it's his left thumb he's shoved up my ass. It's his right hand that he shoves under me, pressing middle finger to clit and gauging the pressure as I squirm on his cock. He seems to know it instinctively. He starts rubbing as he fucks me, drawing out his cock until the thick head nudges my G-spot, then he tips it at just the right angle to get a moan as he increases pressure on my clit. Then he slowly glides down into me, ceasing when the moaning stops. He draws back. He rubs more firmly, more gently, based on how loud my cries get.

Soon it's obvious he's found the spot.

I claw at the sheets. I grab a pillow that smells like him and shove it in my mouth to keep from screaming. I scream anyway. He teases me right to the edge and leaves me there hurting.

Then he pulls it all away: his cock and thumb pop out of me, and his hand abandons my clit. He backs away from the bed. He just leaves me hanging there, ready to come but not allowed.

"All right," he says. "Now you can undress for me."

I'm red all over, but my face and my tits feel hottest. I drop onto the bed and squirm around like mad tearing off my clothes. The little sundress I've worn wouldn't be hard to get off if I could make my hands work, but I can't. Dion stands by the bed and lets me fumble and struggle. I finally kick the dress away, hurling it into a sodden lump on the floor. I pull off my panties and bra and reach out to him desperately, grab his hands and shove him into the bed.

I don't know why I need to give him head just then—I just need to. Maybe it's because with my severe oral performance anxiety, I won't do it if I have to think about it, and right now I'm too crazy with lust to think about anything but pleasuring his cock. I kneel next to the bed, coax his legs apart, and go down on him eagerly, wrapping my lips around his dick. I taste my sex. I suck him hungrily, eyes closed, the feel of his big smooth cock feeling very much like heaven against my tongue and lips and into my throat.

I see a flash and look up. Dion is taking phone cam pics.

I blush a little. I remember that I made him promise me he would. "Something to remember me by," I told him, in one of my very dirty moods.

I keep sucking him, letting him hold my long hair out of the way with one hand while he guides me into a position so he can get shots of his cock, of my face, of my lips parted around his shaft and my tongue swirling around his glistening cockhead. I lower my mouth to his balls and lick those, flashes blinding me over and over again. He punches buttons. I work my way back to his tip in a loving slurp and start making love to the head. More flashes. I know my makeup is ruined, but I've never felt hotter. As crazy as it sounds, I've never felt more beautiful.

"Your husband's name is Rick, isn't it?"

I look up at him. "What?"

Dion holds my hair and positions his cock against my cheek.

"Rick. That's your husband, right?"

I realize he's holding *my* phone, not his.

I smile wanly.

"Oh, my god," I say. "You're not—"

"Come on," says Dion brightly, aiming my phone at me. Again. "Smile for the camera. Don't you think your husband wants to know how much fun you're having?"

I moan softly, arousal instantly dominating every cell in my body. I've never been this turned on. I feel drunk. I feel confused. I feel as if every conscious thought has been blasted out of my head and replaced with sudden need for Dion's cock, as he humiliates and degrades my beloved husband.

"Let's see some tongue," says Dion.

I obey him. I don't know why, but I do. I'm going crazy with lust. I want his cock everywhere. In me, on me. I want his come all over me. I want his brutal camera to drink in every image of me sucking his cock. I want Dion to send them to Rick for him to stare at in disbelief.

I resume sucking Dion's huge cock eagerly, wetly, looking up into the periodic flash of the camera. Every now and then, Dion turns the phone around to show me my image with his dick in my mouth—and to show me the speed dial he's just thumbed into the phone. He makes me watch as he sends it to Rick. And then he turns it around and takes more pictures.

I've gone delirious. I'm going *crazy*. I want Dion's cock like I've never wanted anything in my life. My pussy drips down my thighs, my mounting arousal fueled by betrayal. It isn't long before Dion has to pull me off his cock, panting, to prevent me from making him pop.

Dion pulls me up onto the bed and plants me on my hands and knees. He spanks me. I'm surprised at first, but why didn't I expect it. He knows what this does to me. I've told him a thousand times online, on the phone. He spanks me again, harder. Harder. Still harder. Then the phone cam flashes and he shows me the pic: his big red handprint dark red on my pink pale ass, and Rick's name in speed dial.

Dion sends it. I whimper.

He gets behind me and mounts me. I cry out as he penetrates me. This time I know it won't take his hand to make me come. I'm almost there the second he's inside me. The flash goes off a half dozen times.

He tells me, "Turn around. Face the camera, baby."

I do it. I show him my face, pink with pleasure, while he positions the camera to get a shot of his big cock violating me—and my face looking into the camera as it does.

He does a hell of a job. He shows me the picture. He shows me Rick's name, just in case after dozens of pictures I've decided to wonder if he'll really do it. I see the MESSAGE SENT icon.

Then Dion fucks my ass.

I hear myself moaning, "OhGodOhGodOhGodOhGod," somewhat pathetically, as Dion's huge cock opens me up.

He says, "Oh, Jolie—that's too good to pass up. Let's share that with Rick, shall we? Let me get one more, and—"

The flash goes off. He grabs my hair and tips my head back and shows it to me: his cock breaching my ass, his dark red palm print still upon my cheek. He sends it to Rick right in front of my face.

Then he hits DIAL.

"OhGodOhGodOhGod," I moan incoherently, unable to conceive of what I'm doing as Dion puts the phone to my face and starts rhythmically working his cock in and out of my ass.

"Darling," moans Rick, desperate. "What are you doing? I've been getting these texts—"

"I'm getting fucked, baby," I moan. "I'm getting fucked in the ass. God, it's so fucking good—baby, I'm sorry, I'm getting fucked by a stranger, I'm cheating on you, I'm cheating on you, I'm betraying you, I'm unfaithful, I'm a bad girl, badbadbadbad—"

And then I come, screaming, my eyes rolling back in my head. My hips start working. I shove myself back and forth on Dion's cock. I feel the weight of his body bearing me down as he orders me to come harder for him, and I do. I come harder and harder and harder and harder until I'm screaming into the phone as Dion's cock plunges deep into my ass.

Then Dion groans and pulls out, tips me off the bed and onto my knees. He eases me back and plants his cock over my bare, sweaty tits, over the pearl necklace my husband gave me not an hour before.

As Dion moans loudly in pleasure, I stroke his cock until he shoots all over my anniversary present.

I tell Rick, in case he needs a play-by-play: "He's coming on me, baby, he's fucking coming on my tits. He's coming all over your anniversary present..."

And Rick lets out a long, low groan that tells me he's just shot his load as well.

Dion kills the call so he can send Rick one last picture: my well-spanked cheeks spread wide to display my opened asshole, moist with his spit and my pussy juices.

What is it about men? They love to show off our orifices after they've been fucked. Something about proving "I was here." It never did much for me.

But it did a lot for Rick, I'd find out later.

A lot for Rick. That's the picture he beats off to most, when I'm not around. Or when I am, sometimes.

For me, it's never the pictures. It's always the way it made me feel.

Dirty. Wrong. Evil. Perverse. Like the worst wife in the world, and the very best, all at the same time.

Because Rick had been begging for it.

I won't say it was an anniversary present, exactly. I knew it was possible that Dion would take me up on my strong suggestion that Sunday would be perfect. We had been trying to coordinate schedules for weeks, ever since we both got our batteries of tests back from the clinic. I even had my own copy, complete with a photo of Dion's ID, as he had one of mine. How's that for the right kind of cheating?

But beyond that, I won't say any of it was planned. I had no idea he'd make me wait to come, for instance, after I'd so thoroughly explained how to get me off. And I had no idea he'd give me what I'd fantasized about more often than anything: a hard fuck from behind before I even got a chance to take my panties off.

But the part about the photos and the phone call, the "exposure" of my cheating and the total humiliation of my hapless husband?

Dion knew all about that, because I'd detailed that filthy fantasy half a dozen times. It was only one of a half-dozen possible games we might play when I finally crossed the threshold from online slutwife to *real* slutwife. But it was definitely my favorite.

I thought Dion might go for it. I kind of *hoped*.

Because Rick had *begged for it*.

Greedy
ERIC EMERSON

The guests are due at ten.

Why so late?

As with everything in matters of this sort, it's been carefully planned out. It's midsummer. The last rays of the sun
still stream across the sky until well after nine in our latitude.
It stays light, or at least sort of half-gray, until at least nine-
thirty. And it simply wouldn't do for a married couple to host
a daytime gang bang.

It's not so much that we're worried the neighbors will
notice. It's more that the energy's just all wrong. Beach party
gang bang at noon? Sure. Poolside gang bang, teatime? Check.
Summer camp gang bang, just after morning church services?
Mas oui! But a house party suburban slutwife gang bang in the
daytime, or even the soft fading light of early evening?

Not a damn chance. It's late night or nothing.

Very few of the preparations were your doing, though

every detail was agreed upon. But they were my suggestions, because I'm the expert here.

It was part of the excitement for me that I clean the house, buy the beer and the ice and the porn while you went to the spa all day and got mud-bathed and avocado-scrubbed while sipping champagne. You needed a pedicure. You needed a mani-cure. You needed a fresh set of candy-red nails to break as you rake them down the back of a stranger plunging into you.

In any event, I've done my husbandly duty. The place is immaculate and prepared just so for the scene. Three TVs in the living room play different porn scenes: oral, anal, gang bang. An Office Depot sign-holder on the coffee table features a computer printout saying: SUIT YOURSELF! Beside it sit ten or twelve other porn DVDs, in case our guests should want spanking, bukkake, lesbian videos. Atop the stack of DVDs sits the remote control. Our sofas are draped with sheets.

Since we'll need the bathtub, there's a big metal bucket of ice chilling with beer in the garage. I make cocktails in the kitchen. If a guest wants a beer, all he has to do is snap his fingers, and you'll get it for him. At least until the proceedings begin—thereafter, I'll get his beer.

This isn't because it's my fantasy to wait hand and foot on strangers as they fuck my wife. It's so you and I, between the two of us, can monitor just how much each man is slurping down. A drunk gang bang is a hazardous gang bang. But a very slightly tipsy one is dandy.

Everything's ready.

And you? You look glorious. I picked out your outfit specially for tonight. Packed into the sluttiest snap-crotch teddy $127.50 can buy at the mall, your body looks perfect.

And your face is made up just right for your role of the slut. I should know: I made it up for you. Every stroke of the bright red lipstick, every brush of the blush, every touch of mascara was all laid on by your loving husband as he prepared you to be ravished by eight men. I even gently eased your cherry-red pumps onto your sheer-stockinged feet and kissed your toes as I slid the buckles home. The six-inch heels make you walk with your ass half-thrust out; it looks like you're begging for it.

The guests are due at ten. They start showing up at nine-fifty, dressed in coats and ties—my requirement.

You greet each guest warmly at the door, shying back into the shadows of the mood-lit house, away from the prying eyes of the neighbors. You let him inside, give him a hug. If he wants to grope you, you let him do that—up to and including giving your nipples a wet, sucking kiss, sliding fingers into your cunt, or even caressing your ass a bit. You might even grope the front of his pants a little, rubbing his cock till it's hard.

Then you play hard to get, leaving him grunting and wanting.

"Not until everyone's here," you tell him.

Then you take his coat and hang it in the closet. You lead each guest by the hand into the living room, where he's installed in a chair or on the couch to watch porn while you collect his drink order, get it from me in the kitchen, and walk back with the beer or the cocktail on a tray, even putting down a coaster and a napkin so as not to muss our table.

You bend over as you put the drink down. If one of the men reaches up and feels you, you push back against him and moan. He always finds you wet. Once a few of them try that, the others get the idea. Every time you bring back a drink, you bend over emphatically so your guests can finger you. Some try your ass. Most like your cunt. One tries to guide you into his lap, your face leaving lipstick traces on his gray slacks.

"Not till everyone's here," you tell him, caressing his dick and then leaving him to stare after you in hunger while you fetch another drink, or get the door, or fix your lipstick.

Or slip into the kitchen to kiss me hard and stroke my cock through my pants.

"God, I'm so fucking wet," you keep telling me.

"Having fun?"

"Having *fun*," you keep saying emphatically, and race back to take care of your guests—and, in so doing, tease the *hell* out of them.

The fiction of the scene is that you're their servant. That's as much your fantasy as mine, but it has little to do with reality. In reality, which one of us is the servant would take a year of psychoanalysis to figure out. I think it's me. But maybe it's you. You always wanted this, but you never thought it could be real. Even in the swinger's community, a true, happy, drama-free gang bang is a relative rarity. Lucky for you the man you fell in love with had two previous girlfriends who were even bigger sluts than you.

But you're working on it.

Once you've had eight, or possibly ten, or just maybe twelve hard cocks inside you tonight, you'll have a whole new claim on the label "slut."

That number—eight or ten or twelve—could be problematic.

The number of guests was a matter of some disagreement

between you and me. You were convinced that when offered the chance to participate in a gang bang with the hottest blonde slutwife in six counties, your average red-blooded straight man would never suffer the exhaustive screening process—interviews, blood test, even a photocopy of his identification—and then flake.

"*Au contraire*," I told you. "Just wait. You'll see. I don't understand it any more than you do. Men are chicken. Some might be cheating on their wives or something. They'll get cold feet. They'll back out. It's nothing personal."

You'll have a hard time not taking it personally, however. I think any woman would. But lucky for you, you'll have lots of cock tonight to help you through the lonely pain of having a few men not show up.

I said twelve or fourteen would be good.

You wanted eight.

"Come on," you said. "No need to be *greedy*."

"It's not greedy," I told you. "It's *prudent*."

We screened twelve, figuring you'd get your eight and no more.

When the tenth man shows up, about ten-fifteen, I shrug.

"Sorry," I tell you as I mix him a Tom Collins in the kitchen. "I guess you're even hotter than I thought you were."

You wink at me.

"It's all right," you say. "I think I *do* want to be a little greedy, after all."

It's time to get started.

I turn off the porn.

I can tell you're a bit nervous. What woman wouldn't be?

You stall by going around the room and freshening the drinks, answering the groping, reaching hands with wiggles and caresses of your own. The hands pinch your nipples as you pass and slide up under the crotch of your teddy, caressing your shaved puss. They stroke your smooth thighs. They spank your ass lightly.

They're more than a little reckless; almost all of them are hard. If it wasn't for me, I know, you'd be truly scared. The fact that I'm six-two and used to play football helps. You're not the type to like particularly big or particularly rough-looking guys, so these are your average garden-variety guys who want to fuck another man's wife in a gang bang— computer programmers, lawyers, college boys. Any assholes got themselves unceremoniously bounced before the in-person interview. These guys are gentlemen on some level, or at least as much a gentleman as one can be when you're about to plow a stranger's wife.

I sit in an armchair near the kitchen, watching the scene. There are three guys on each of our two facing sofas, two more in wingbacks, two more in wooden chairs from the kitchen. You shoot me a glance. You're radiating excitement as you thrust your ass back against a groping hand and eagerly start to suck on the fingers of another guy. Two more are pawing at your tits. They get their hands under the top of your teddy. They caress and pinch your nipples. You moan around the stranger's fingers, taking them deep enough that you start to gag a little bit. Then you're not gagging any more—you've taken two or three fingers into your throat, easily.

That's enough of an invitation. The guy with the hands

gets off the couch and starts to unbuckle his belt. You take over, your hands moving with expert confidence. His zipper goes down in moments. You take his big, long pale cock out and slide it in your mouth while, behind you, another man unsnaps the crotch of your teddy and guides his cock inside you.

You've been practicing for weeks, doing deep knee bends and stretches. You shove your ass in the air to take his cock in your cunt while you bend low to suck the other man's cock. Your hands drift out and find the cocks of the two men groping your tits. You open their pants without even glancing over. You get their cocks in your hands and start stroking.

It's a glorious sight, you bent over far, sucking, stroking, and getting fucked. But even with weeks of stretching and practicing, you can't bend over like that forever. After several long minutes of hard fucking and moaning, the men you're servicing pull back and politely let some of the others have turns. Two pull you into their laps, face down, and you grope their cocks from their pants, stroking and jerking and licking and sucking as another props your hips up high and fucks you from behind. Two more lean in to feel your tits as you suck. Any reluctance these guys might have had to be in physical contact with each other seems to have vanished. They don't mind as long as they can get close to you.

I crane my head to make sure you're enjoying yourself. I catch a glimpse of your face, drool and ruined lipstick running everywhere as you come up from a hard cock, smiling and laughing. Suspended between two laps, you switch from one to the other and drop down and lick balls while you stroke the other man's cock. The one fucking you grunts and climaxes, thunderously. You moan loudly as he comes in you. He holds the base of the condom and pulls out. Another takes his place, condom already at the ready.

Someone groping your tits rips at your teddy. They've already been told the expensive garment is a lost cause. They have, in fact, been invited to ruin it. The teddy gets torn off, shredded. One of the men unsnaps your garters so the fishnet stay-ups remain in place on your glorious legs. Isn't that conscientious of him?

Another one is fucking you now, his condom-sheathed cock shoved deep inside you while you moan and buck against him. One of the men in your mouth climaxes, and you slurp it up audibly. Another comes in your hand and shoots his load across your face. You lick and suck and lap and writhe in their arms.

While they're all over you on the couch, I move the drinks from the coffee table to the mantle. Then I get the foam-rubber pad and the extra sheet from the closet and lay it on the sturdy coffee table.

With only the slightest suggestion from me, they move you over onto the now-padded coffee table, stretching you out on it and spreading your legs. It's just high enough that the one who first rolls on a condom and crouches over you can easily slide in your well-lubed cunt while your head hangs easily off the far end. Tipped down like that, it will be easy for you to deep-throat. You open wide, and three men in turn slide their cocks down your throat as the fourth crouches over you, fucking, and you jerk two more off with your hands. I crane my head to watch. Each man who throat-fucks you takes his time, letting you inhale, gulp, swallow, choke a little, struggle, and then take him down your throat. Seeing that, others want to get into the act. I think you must deep-throat eight of the ten in that unbelievably hot-looking position, and I crowd in to watch every sliding cock go down your throat.

The man fucking you comes. He pulls out holding the condom. Another takes his place.

I hand him a vibrator, the plug trailing a long, brown extension cord.

I've decided it's time for you to come. You have no objection. He seems to know his way around a vibrator and applies it to your clit with firm pressure. You cry out as he enters you. He starts fucking you hard, vibrator pressed to your clit. Men trade off sliding their cocks into your mouth, fucking your tipped-back face as you get fucked and dish out hand jobs. It isn't long before you let out a grunting yell around the cock you're sucking. The one in your mouth pulls out so everyone can hear you come. You come hard, shuddering all over and making the coffee table rattle.

As soon as you're finished, they're back to taking turns with your face, and the man fucking you is back at that, too, vibe discarded. He fucks you hungrily, intent on his own pleasure.

One of them lingers in your throat, slowly fucking your face as you grunt, gasp, and moan. He slaps his cock across your face lightly and you maul at it, capturing it between your full, lipstick-smeared lips and thrusting yourself onto it. You let him fuck your face for a long series of thrusts, until he gasps and pulls out and strokes his cock off on your face. You stick your tongue out and lap at his jizz. Two men in your hands also grunt and groan and start humping against your grasp, their cocks lubed with pre-come, spit, and sweat. They shoot all over your tits. You smear it in and lick it off your fingers as the one in your pussy comes. Four more men are there to use you. For one, it's not his first time—but then, who can blame him? It's a gang bang, and there's plenty of you to go around. What's wrong with being a little greedy?

When the coffee table starts to creak and moan with the weight and the hard heavy thrusting, I spread out a blanket and you move to the floor, face-down, ass-up, moaning as you jerk and stroke and slurp and suck and get fucked.

It two a.m. before you're finally sated. Or maybe it's that they're sated—you've worn them out. My cock's been throbbing hard the whole time, and I could have joined in any time I wanted to. But that's not the point.

When they're finished, a few want to shower. Others dress, still sticky with your sweat and your juice and their come. At least half of them say "Thank you" to me, looking bewildered, like they're thinking, "What does a man say to the husband in a slutwife gang bang?"

I respond by grasping their hands in a warm, friendly handshake, both our hands sticky with come, lube, and pussy.

"Thanks, man. Hope to see you next time."

It's fucking ludicrous, to treat something this sacred like a friendly neighborhood get-together. Or is it?

I don't care. You're squirming on the blanket, hips still moving, gone mad with the craziness of it all. Your hair is matted with come. Your face is sticky with it. Your pussy pours juice. Come runs in rivulets down your belly.

I pick you up in my arms and carry you to bed.

* * *

I'm going to bathe you, yes, but all in good time. We've got business first.

I pull back the covers and lay you out in our bed, soiling clean sheets with come. You lay there, spread and squirming and moaning. You're naked. The shoes and the stockings and every last shred of your teddy are long gone. You're bare. Your body drips.

I take off my clothes and make love to you tenderly. You're completely relaxed, almost half-conscious, your cunt and your tits and your mouth and your throat raw with use. I go as gently as I can, and when I enter you—without protection, of course—you rise up to meet me even though I can feel the swollen roughness of your well-used sex. You still feel tight.

I fuck you very gently, but there's not much I can do to hold myself back.

I last a minute at most.

You sense my climax arriving. You wrap your come-slick legs around me and pull me close and hard onto you. You grip me and moan as I come in your pussy. You caress me. You sigh.

You've got one last orgasm in you, I've decided. I lick my way down your body, tasting other men's come.

It's only lube in your pussy, of course—weirdly sweet lube mingled with my own come. I lick it tenderly, well aware that you're hypersensitive. I go slow, take my time, and take *your* time. You're exhausted, but you prop yourself up in the bed and look down at me, gazing into my eyes as my face works between your spread thighs. I lap at your cunt and then, when it's time, I lick up to your clit.

I know your body well enough to make you come even

when you swear you can't. This time, you don't swear you can't. Your exhaustion has given way to a superhuman kind of need. You want to give me this. You want to grant me this last chance to please you.

Your thighs close tight around my head as you explode. You ride me as you come. I keep working my tongue on your clit until you've clawed away the contour sheets, and they go bunched and moist off under your back—until your moaning turns to whimpers.

Then I kiss my way back up your come-soiled body and kiss you gently on the mouth.

The last of the ritual has to wait, I guess. I had planned to bathe you gently in warm water, with sponges and flower-scented body wash. But you're snoring before I can even discuss it with you.

So I stretch out next to you and feel the sticky warmth of your come-covered body against mine.

I kiss your neck and fall asleep.

Moneymaker

ISABELLE ROSS

You slam the motel room door and shove me up hard against it. My breath quickens. I watch in trembling fear as you reach around me and lift the chain lock. You put it in the notch and slide it home.

"I'll need the money first," I say, my voice trembling.

You push up hard against me, your cock stiff in leather pants. You brush my bottle-blonde hair out of my face and say: "You'll need the money *never*. You work for *me* now."

I open my mouth as if to scream, but you get your hand across my face. You tell me, "Shhhhh" and put your hand up my skirt, squeeze my asscheeks, and kick my legs open.

You shove your hand into my panties and feel my cunt. I'm shaved and wet. You start fingering my pussy.

"How long you been turning tricks?" you ask me.

"A while," I say.

You shove two fingers into me. I gasp and moan.

"Bullshit," you say. "I know what a well-used cunt feels like, and this ain't it. You're fresh, darling. Not for long, but you're fresh. I get to sample you. Now tell Daddy the truth. How long you been turning tricks?"

My voice shakes. "You're my first," I say.

"I doubt that." You spank me, pull my hair. "Nice sweet college girl. Thought she'd dabble a little? Make some extra cash between internships?"

"Something like that," I say.

You pull my hair and make me squeal. You smack my ass.

"You lose that smart mouth or I'll bury it," you tell me. "You got a boyfriend?"

"Fiancé."

"He know what you are?"

"Yeah," I nod.

"He know you're a whore?"

"Uh-huh," I nod.

"He know you suck strange cocks for money?"

"Yes." I'm breathing hard now, increasingly aroused.

"He know you take strange cocks in your holes?"

I nod and moan.

"He know you take dick in your ass?"

I shake my head fervently. "I don't. I don't do Greek!"

You spank me, making me grunt in rising pain. "You do now. He get off on it?"

I gasp: "Who?"

"See? You're forgetting about him already. Good girl. I mean your fiancé. He get off on fucking a whore?"

I whimper. You spank me again. You shove your hand around my body, up my skirt, into my panties, and finger me hard, grinding your stiffening cock against my ass.

"Kinda," I say.

"Sounds like more than 'kinda,'" you say, rubbing my clit. I moan and rub back against you.

You drag me away from the door and shove me over the bed, pinning me under you. You kick my legs open wide again and hold me there, spread and exposed, half on the bed with my high-heeled shoes dangling. You spank me five or six more times, making me wriggle and fight. You pull my hair and spank me harder in response. You start to finger me.

I'm wetter than when you started, much wetter.

"Your boyfriend the one who sends you out on the street to whore?"

"Fiancé," I correct, and you pull your fingers out of me and spank my ass again, harder than ever this time, maybe ten times, sharp smacks echoing through the small motel room as you do. I cry out as the stinging pain gets too much to take.

You shove your fingers back in my panties and finger me.

"I asked you a question," you say.

"Yes," I say. "He's the one who whores me out."

"You like making money for your man?"

I nod, squirming on your fingers.

"You like making money for your daddy?" you say.

I nod more eagerly, pushing my ass up into the air to fuck myself onto your fingers.

"You like taking strange cock for your daddy? What was your name again?"

"Katrina," I murmur, my words muffled by the pillow I've shoved my face into.

"Oh, don't worry about screaming, Katrina. They hear all

sorts of funny things here. They don't ever call the cops. I asked you if you like taking strange cocks bareback and begging for it up your ass and sucking filthy men's cocks for your big, bad, loving daddy, Katrina. You like all that?"

I throw back my head and gasp and squeal, on the very brink of orgasm. I shake back and forth. I hump on your fingers.

"I asked you a question, Katrina. You like all that? You like being a whore for your daddy?"

"Yes," I manage to choke out, as I fuck myself up against your hand. I'm incredibly close. But you don't let me come.

You pull me off the bed and shove me onto my knees. I kneel there, heaving and panting, as you sit on the bed and unzip your pants.

"Not anymore you don't," you say. "You like doing all those things for *me*. I'm your daddy now, Katrina. That old boyfriend of yours? Mr. Nice Guy? The one who wanted to put a ring on your finger?"

Your zipper comes down and your cock comes out. Holding my hair, you guide my face to your cock and shove it in my mouth.

I know I should fight, but I haven't got it in me. I start sucking obediently, my mouth leaving tracks of cheap red lipstick up and down your pole. As I suck, you hold my hair out of the way so I can't hide from your cold, probing eyes.

You tell me: "Mr. Nice Guy's gone, Katrina. That dick in your mouth right now? That's your new daddy's dick. You whore for *Daddy* now. You walk the streets for *Daddy* now, Katrina." I keep sucking obediently, hungrily working your cock as I taste the steady drizzle of pre-come leaking onto my tongue. I can hear your voice going weak with the building pleasure. "You're Daddy's little moneymaker now, Katrina. You shake that pretty ass and bring it home for your new daddy. Five dollars for a blow, ten dollars for a fuck, fifteen for Greek. No kissing, no hand jobs, no freebies for the cops, no rough stuff from anyone but me. You got that, Katrina? You're gonna do everything Daddy says, aren't you?"

You pull me off your cock. Drool runs down onto my chin and soaks my tube top. I pant and whimper and heave as you pull my hair and force my head back.

You lean down and spit in my face.

"I asked you a question, Katrina."

I've got the fight back in me. I feel it rising in my belly. I'm going to fight you. I've got everything it takes.

I cock my head and spit back.

I can tell you're surprised by that. You don't expect a reluctant whore. I'm such a horny little cunt day in, day out, you have to practically keep me on a leash. I'm so compliant you can leave a note like TUNA CASSEROLE on the fridge, and I'll have it served up steaming with a side of I'm-not-wearing-any-underwear by the time you get home from your Post-Colonial Governmental Intercessions seminar.

And I'm *far* from a smart-assed little masochist.

But I'm a whore tonight. I'm your whore. You're trying to make me your whore. You've got to break me.

So you don't lose your temper. You just grab me, hair and wrist, and haul me over your lap.

Spank.

I squeal.

"You wanna play dirty?"

Spank.

You yank my very short, very tight skirt up over my ass, exposing the whisper of cheap lace that pass as my panties. You yank those down my thighs, to the point where they reach the tops of my stockings.

Spank. Spank. Spank.

You yank my panties away, popping my garters. One clasp rattles against the nightstand. You shove my panties to my knees and spank me harder.

Your cock rubs against me. I writhe. My tube top is gone, on my shoulders or my belly or wherever. You spank me again and I squirm. Harder. I fight.

I'm squirming too much for your taste, I guess. You get both your big, leather-jacketed arms around me and hold me tightly in position over your lap, hammering down with your open palm while I cry out. When I try to close my legs you pin those open, too. You're like an octopus, pinning me everywhere I can move.

And then you're on my sweet spot, spanking rhythmically, forcing me to orgasm.

Maybe you've finally realized why I spat on you.

That was a mean trick, bastard, to get me all close and then make me give you head. I could already taste your pre-come. You would have popped in my mouth in another ten seconds. And then where would we be?

You give it to me slowly, like a maestro building toward the crescendo.

You're in total control.

Tipped over your lap, my ass in the air, my legs spread, my sweet spot resonating right into my clit with every hard blow of your palm, I'm in total surrender.

I strain desperately against your weight, squirming and fighting and arching my back, trying to stop it from happening. That's why it happens so *good*.

I come.

You ride me through it, spanking me, holding me down against your lap, tight.

Then you shove me onto the bed and haul my hips up, forcing my ass into the air. You grab my panties and pull one side of them off over one fishnet stocking and one high-heeled shoe, leaving the stiff, sex-soaked slip of cheap lace dangling from my other ankle. You spread my legs.

You shove your cock into me.

My cunt still spasms as you enter me, your big cockhead stretching me open. You slide in deep. I gasp and shove myself onto you, grinding my hips back and forth.

"Understand, Katrina?"

"Yes, Daddy," I moan.

You start to fuck me as rough as you can manage, which isn't actually very rough, because you're struggling to hold back. You're going to come. You want to pound me, but another three or four thrusts and you'll be gone.

I take this as the highest form of compliment. Most nights you'll last for hours if I give you the chance. Tonight you can't even fuck me properly for fear of blowing your load.

So I think fast: "Daddy," I moan. "Please don't make me do Greek."

You pull your cock out of me. I gasp and moan like I've just been deflated.

"Go get the lube," you say.

I'm not sure how to play this. It's not a typical experiment. Anal sex is something I do only with an enormous amount of pre-planning and the promise of bubble baths and preferably Porsches. It's good when it's good, but it takes a lot out of me. I don't know why I said it. I just did. Because it was hot. Because you were in control, and I was afraid it was going to end with you coming already. So I escalated things.

Do I break up the scene and say, "Just kidding," or do I do it? Do I go through with it? Do I let you fuck me in the ass?

When you get tired of waiting, your voice is heavy and heated, hinting at anger.

"Daddy gave you an *order*, Katrina."

There's something deeply humiliating about being forced to get up and go get the lube so you can fuck me in the ass. I do so under the loud protest of my more sensible self. I go to the little hot pink plastic purse I stuffed full of condoms and lube and sweaty $5 bills.

I dump it all on the cracked counter and pick out the little tube of KY.

My face feels hot as I bring it back to the bed and give it to you.

It's deeply degrading to hand over the lube you're going to use to plow my ass to show my submission to you. The fact that I could end it all with a word or even a look doesn't make it any less degrading. It just makes the degradation something I can handle, something positive. I don't understand it any more than you do, or than *anyone* would.

You pluck the lube from my hand, push me away, and gesture at me.

"Take those off," you say.

You mean my clothes. What is there left to take off? I have to grope to find the tube top. It's at an angle around my rib cage. The dog collar stays. The clasps of the garters have been popped on both sides. My fishnets hang limp and bunched at my calves. The skirt is just a strip of fabric perched atop my hips.

But I wouldn't dream of disobeying you, now that I've accepted you're about to own me utterly.

I kick off my high-heeled shoes and fishnets, pull down the skirt, and pull the tube top over my head.

Then I put my shoes back on.

I perch next to you and say meekly, "How do you want me, Daddy?"

Your only answer is a hand in my hair and an arm around my waist. You spill me doggie-style across the bed again and open my legs with your knees. Your mouth descends, unexpectedly, between my cheeks. I feel your tongue wriggling into my ass, and I cry out in shock. This was the last thing I expected. You've never done this before.

It tightens me at first, but after a few minutes of the soft, warm sensation of your tongue caressing my asshole, I start to relax. You take your time, your tongue swirling and surging and opening me up: Daddy's Little Moneymaker. With the weight of your body and the hard thrusts of your tongue, you work me from a face-down, ass-up position into a fully prone one. Then I feel your tongue replaced by your finger, slick with lube. Then another finger. Then both at once.

Then your cock. I let out a gasp. I whimper. You give me time for my ass to get used to your cock, an inch at a time, until you're mostly in me.

Then you fuck me.

I've never enjoyed anal sex the way I do tonight, taking it spread and helpless on a cheap motel bedspread from my new pimp, my new Master, my daddy. You hold me down and fuck me slowly, until you're sure I can take it. Until I beg for more.

Then you pound me hard, till I beg you to come.

The smooth slick feeling of your come in my ass is humiliating and liberating. I lay underneath you long after you've finished.

You kiss the back of my neck and tell me you love me.

And that's it. It's over. You've put a leash on me. I'm your whore.

Forever after, I'll be Daddy's little moneymaker.

My Number One Fan

SARAH SANDS

Something was up. There was just something about the way Chloe hugged me when I walked into the bar. She held me a little too long, a little too close, a bit too reluctant to give up her grasp on my shoulders. Her hands even lingered a tad along my arms. They gave me goose bumps.

Chloe and I were not what I would call *really* close, which is why what happened later would surprise me so much. Sometimes you do things and they just, like, happen, almost without your input. And Chloe's energy that night seemed to invite such a "something."

The feeling creeped me out a little.

I think even Amy, usually clueless to sexual matters, noticed the energy. It would have been kind of hard not to, since it was just the three of us. Every Thursday night, the patio at Rick's is routinely crowded with our friends. But this was the week of Burning Man, and no one was around except

Amy, who couldn't get off work, and Chloe, famously poor after her layoff, and me. I was in a new relationship, or a relatively new relationship, so I didn't feel like going out of town. I was having too much fun as it was.

In fact, I had brought Sean to Rick's about a month ago. He proved a big hit with all my friends. My bringing him there meant it was serious. He'd wanted to come tonight, but he said cryptically that he had "important business," which did terrible things to my attention span. I couldn't stop thinking about him, wondering what he was up to.

Amy and Chloe and I chatted. No matter what I said, Chloe hung on my every word. I didn't get it. I hadn't been waxed or preened or puffed or had a nose job or a tit job or tried a new perfume since last week, when Chloe was friendly enough but not all over me.

When Amy said she'd get the next round, Chloe, the broke one, practically threw $40 at her and said, "Add a round of bourbon, Ames?"

"Oh, I'm driving," said Amy.

"Well, then, Sarah and me?"

"All right," I said defiantly. "I'm game. I'm on the bus."

"We can take a cab," said Chloe. "Since we're going the same direction."

I looked her over suspiciously.

"Yeah," I said. "Apparently."

Amy left the table.

I drew a breath to tell Chloe I thought she was making Amy uncomfortable. Before I could utter a word or even get all my breath in, Chloe was leaning forward and pawing my denim-covered arms.

"Oh. My. God," she said. "Ohmigod. Ohmigod. Ohmigod, ohmigod, ohmigod, ohmigod, ohmigod, who's your biggest fan?"

My mouth popped shut. I gave her the "Crazy much?" look.

"Who's your number one fan? You sick *perv!*"

It still took me a second. I buried my face in my hands.

"Ohmigod, so fucking good," she said. "Hawt! Hawt! Hawt! Hawt! Hawt! Every word true, Sarah? Every word true, like you promised?"

I *had* promised.

I said, "Yeah." My voice sounded squeaky and uncomfortable.

"He *did* that to you?"

I shrugged, turning seven shades of red. I nodded.

"When?"

"Recently," I said nervously.

Chloe looked excited, but as red as I was, she was probably twice as embarrassed. After all, I was the one who had written it.

I'm not saying I object. I'm not a shy person, really. Just *private*. That's why when I started a blog detailing my sexual adventures with Sean, I never even thought of doing it bareback. Which is to say, without a pseudonym, or at least the barest hint of one.

I was Sleazy Slut Sara, without the "h." The explicitly detailed stories were true to my pseudonym, in every way except the fact that it was mostly with Sean that I fucked around. But there were exceptions. The boywhore in Las Vegas. The stripper in L.A. The man at the glory hole...mmmm...the glory hole...

The stories were true, or at least I *said* they were true. In a way I took every liberty, but in another I took *no* liberties, owing to Sean's overwhelming fucking *amazingness*. And mine, if you must know.

The blog was not secured. Strangers were welcome to read every detail of every filthy, whorish thing I'd let Sean do to me in all the thousands upon thousands of words Sleazy Slut Sara had posted. But people who knew me *weren't*. Unless they were. I'd told a few—a very few—of my friends about my sex blog. If they could handle it, if they needed it…or I thought they did…I gave it to them.

Which was sort of my thinking when it came to Chloe. Though she was not a *close* friend, exactly, over the three years we'd run in the same social circle, we'd naked-acid-hot-tubbed and braided each others' hair and shared tips on giving head and, far more important, tips on *getting* head.

Which is not to say I hadn't basically done the same things with Amy, but Amy could be sort of a prude. Chloe had told me a few dirty adventures over the years.

So when I'd started the blog about four months ago, Chloe was one of the very few acquaintances I shared the URL with in my initial rush of creative energy. I'd all but forgotten I had…until now.

Chloe was breathing hard and giggling, desperately nervous. I frowned.

"Which one are you talking about?"

She made a shocked sound.

"The new one," she said. "Of *course*!"

Oh, shit. The new one. The new one. I reddened deeper. I got so embarrassed I had to hide my face. I couldn't look her in the eye. Chloe giggled. She tittered. She reached across and rubbed my arm and said, "It's all right, baby. Here come our drinks. We'll talk later."

The whole exchange had taken like two minutes, if that. Amy is hot. She gets service fast at hipster bars. Besides, it was Burning Man. There was practically no one in the Mission.

Amy brought back a pitcher of beer and a tray with two double shots of bourbon. Amy filled her glass only half way. "I think I'll be heading out, soon," she said. We made small talk until she did, and then Chloe and I ordered another round... and another.

"Did you negotiate it first?"

"Um...in detail," I said—not entirely true.

"Total *ravishment* fantasy, right?" She looked me in the eye, her face close. She formed her lips around the words, aiming them right at me, not a sound coming out of her mouth: "I mean...total *rape*."

"Um, yeah," I said. "Rape *fantasy*."

"*Rape* fantasy," said Chloe excitedly.

"Rape *fantasy*," I said, feeling my temperature rising.

She leaned very close to me and repeated: "*Rape* fantasy."

I shifted uncomfortably.

"*Rape* fantasy," I said.

She seemed satisfied.

"You're cool with that?" she asked desperately.

"Um," I said. "Duh!"

"It was your idea!"

"Totally," I said, feeling drunk. "Every detail."

"But he takes over. He just grabs you in the dark and... *does* you."

"Yeah," I said.

"Holds you down, bends you over, lets you struggle, lets you tire yourself out, and then…"

"Um," I said. "Um, um, um, um—"

"And when he flipped you over and—"

"Um!" I interrupted. "Embarrassed much?"

"I'm sorry. I just never thought people really did stuff like that."

I shrugged. "Yeah…we do."

I nodded drunkenly. Our eyes locked into each other, and I could have kissed her then.

"Whew," Chloe said. "Well, if you ever—" She caught herself and got very embarrassed. "I mean, I'm not…I know you guys are committed and all. I'm not saying…" She was red as a beet.

The trick was not to think about it too much.

"Sean would go for it," I blurted.

Chloe breathed hard.

My cell phone buzzed in my jean jacket pocket.

I took it out.

Sean had texted me: COME HOME.

I typed back: I'M DRNUK.

Sean: SLUT. JUST ***ASKING*** FOR IT.

My muscles tightened. I felt the snugness of my jacket just a little more acutely for a moment.

I smiled at Chloe.

"Um, or not," she shrugged, nervously. "I mean, our friendship—I wouldn't want to—"

For fifteen seconds, Chloe's mouth spewed a tangle of words making next to no sense: "commitment," "single," "while

I'm not in a relationship," "totally no strings attached," "I'm not a homewrecker," "just that, I mean, if you guys are—"

I stopped her with my hand on her shoulder.

"Chloe!" I said, laughing softly.

She stopped and stared at me, ashamed and nervous, breathing hard, excited.

My cell phone buzzed.

Text from Sean: *****BEGGING*****

My jeans felt tight. My insides felt tight. I wanted to crawl out of my skin, in both a good way and a bad way, all at once.

"We'll talk," I told her.

It wouldn't happen, not that night, because it hadn't yet been written down. What did happen was a cab ride to my place ten blocks away, the two of us leaning slightly closer together than we might have otherwise. Then a kiss, on the lips, and a tiny hint of Chloe's bourbon tongue. Her hand on my stomach, then up, touching my breasts.

"We'll talk,"

"Promise?"

"Yeah."

I got out, went in, and huffed up the stairs as the cab took Chloe on to her condo in the Haight.

My skin felt alive as I unlocked the door. Every part of me felt alive. I was dizzy with liquor. I was high on adrenaline.

I tried to act normal, not knowing what was coming. I did what I'd normally do. I slid off my jacket. I dropped it to the floor. I kicked off my clogs. I unzipped my jeans and pulled them sweat-soaked to my knees and shins and ankles and danced around struggling for a bit trying to get out of them, never turning on the light, because I wouldn't have, normally. This drunk and this late and this horny, I'd climb right in bed and masturbate so fucking hard I'd break furniture.

I finally got the parasite jeans off my feet and headed into the kitchen for the water filter, in my T-shirt and panties.

That's when he took me from behind.

He was hard. Not his cock. His whole body. It was as if, making love to him constantly for six delicious months, I'd never felt the total hardness on his broad-shouldered, powerful frame. His muscles were hard. His hand was tight across my face. His knife felt cold against my collarbone. Fresh from the freezer.

Cold makes it sharper. At least, it feels that way.

The knife was very, very important. Otherwise, why wouldn't I scream? I'm not stupid. I'm not cowardly. I'm not some weak, meaningless, useless, helpless girl, just waiting to be given the gift of forcible ravishment, granted by Man the tender gift of rape. I'm not just *asking for it*.

No one ever is, is she?

"Don't make a sound," he said, drawing the knife down my throat.

But I did make a sound. I couldn't stop myself. It was a whimper of arousal and of pleasure and of terror.

Then the knife was gone. I never saw it again, but it was always there, keeping me silent except for the moans.

He bent me hard over the counter. He *shoved* me. He yanked my underwear aside and entered me *fast*, without time for me to get used to the idea that I was being taken. He didn't need to say what we were both thinking: "She's wet. She's so wet she's dripping. She's so wet she's pouring on his cock. She's a slut. She's a victim. She wants this."

And she did, but *she* didn't. The girl I was playing was helpless and ravished, which is why I fought against the pleasure building in me. And why when I emitted a deep dismayed yell and climaxed on his violent thrusts, he wasn't finished with me. He came in me. Whether he seeded me actually or just put on a really good show, I'll never know, and at the time I didn't even consider. All I knew was a stranger was coming inside me and I was being *soiled*, while my pussy still pulsed from my own orgasm, against which I'd struggled.

He pulled me off the counter. He propped me up with one hand across my mouth and one hand in my hair. He shoved me into the bedroom. I walked funny.

He threw me on the bed and held me down.

I struggled anew, my fear refreshed. Sean is big. He overpowered me. He pulled my panties off and shoved them in my mouth, tore my T-shirt to shreds, and covered my face with it so I was blinded and could smell the scent of my fear. He held me down naked under his big, muscular body and let me fight and fight and fight. He let me tire myself out, just like in the story. He let me fight until I was panting and whimpering and on the verge of tears. Then he let me fight some more, and I did.

Sometimes he laughed. Sometimes he mocked me, saying, "Fight, fight, yeah, go ahead and fight. I'll fuck you however I want, whenever I want, and I'll come back for more tomorrow night. Fight all you want. It makes my dick hard."

The sound of it scared me and broke me and shattered something deep in my soul. It made me see my lover like I never had before: as a man, the kind of man part of me always feared any man could be.

I fought him desperately. Sometimes when he had me

pinned really good with one hand and his knees and his body, he ran his hands all over me, over my tits and my hips and my thighs as I tried to hold my legs together, even though I knew, as Sean knew, that as soon as he wished it he would forcibly spread them.

Then he did.

He held me down and forced my legs open.

I fought, but there was little left in me.

He held me down on the bed and entered me, sharp and hard and brutal in a single thrust.

I moaned.

Pleasure was overcoming my resistance. Every instant I'd resisted had amped my desire up to a fresh new level. Now that he was in me, I was helpless—not just because he had me completely under his physical control, but because I wanted it so much it obliterated every other aspect of my psyche.

He had broken me.

I still resisted, as much as I could. But he took me at a leisurely pace, fucking me slow and deep and making me feel every stroke. He took his time. He used me well on my back, for twenty, thirty minutes, missionary position, until I was good and sore. Then he flipped me, my struggles renewing as he held my face in one pillow and shoved others under my hips. He raised my ass high. He entered me again.

I felt the buzzing.

He had a vibrator.

This part was improv. It could have spoiled everything. What kind of a rapist uses a vibrator on his victim?

The *fantasy* rapist, of course. Which was Sean to a *T*.

I swear I didn't even feel it approaching. I don't ever come in that position. It's far from my favorite. The reason I wrote it into the story is that some part of me still thinks it's humiliating to be fucked on my knees.

It was far more humiliating to come on my knees, even harder than the first time.

I was over on my back again, forced open wide and pinned tight beneath Sean before the spasms stopped. Soaring high on my orgasm, I felt him enter me again. Then the pounding started. Not thrusting. Not stroking. Not fucking. The *pounding* that says, "I'm going to cum, bitch."

He did, and fast. I had a whole complicated section where I begged him not to cum in me and…well, you can read the blog someday, maybe.

He didn't care. He did me fast. He did me hard. He shot his load in me as if I was a tissue.

And the fact that he came so fast was more gratifying to me than anything he'd done so far.

A minute later he was out of me, his soft cock dripping come like my pussy.

He said, "The End."

I buried myself in his arms. I drowned myself in his scent. We both stank like holy hell after what must have been two hours of struggles and fucking. We both smelled like heaven.

He held me and let me heave and pant and gasp and tremble and say, "Thank you, thank you, thank you" to the point where it was stupid. I felt like a dork. He held me anyway.

It had all been spot-on, well, yeah, most of it. The grabbing me, the knife, cold and sharp. The bending me over. The quickness of his taking, without even bothering to undress me, without even pulling my panties off. The shoving me into the bedroom. The struggles, the letting me tire myself out until I was help-less. The panties, the shirt, the turning me over.

The vibrator? Fine, I would give him that. A director can't quite script *everything*. Right?

Especially not when she's in the starring role.

I wanted to tell Chloe. I wanted to call that drunken, crazy slut right away and tell her it really had happened, and that the bland account I'd published online was nothing at all like the real thing. The real thing was a thousand times better. It always was. The fantasy script was laid out in my blog for my man to follow in every filthy detail.

And he made it *better*.

I wanted to tell her, but I couldn't. She couldn't know this was all after-the-fact. She had to think my journal was memoir, not script.

Until I let her star in her own private post, for me to read alone, and then with Sean, because a little coordination would be necessary.

Once I had kissed those bourbon lips and tasted sex...*my sex?*

I'd tell her.

Fantasies are for tomorrow.

It was so late that it became pretty clear we were both going to call in sick, or at least I was. I'd be hung over. Sean was stone sober.

I kissed his chest and said, "Guess what?"

"What?"

"I met my number one fan tonight," I said, softly glowing with writer's pride.

I felt that creative pride even more acutely than I did my seething lust for the hot girl I would soon hand Sean on a platter. I had the story plotted out: invitation, flirtation, seduction, the words to describe her.

"What was that?" Sean smirked. "What'd you say?"

"I met my number one fan tonight," I repeated.

He grabbed my hair and pulled my face to his.

"Fuck, yeah, you did," he said. He kissed me hard.

About the Authors

Living and working in Hampshire, England, **J. HADLEIGH ALEX** is keen to explore branches of fiction that breach boundaries, to tell stories that tease taboos, and to write without limitation or fear. His erotic podcast Deranged Imagination can be found at derangedimagination.blogspot.com.

SKYE BLACK's darker erotic work has appeared in several Usenet newsgroups and on the websites Necromantic.com and Noirotica.net.

M. CHRISTIAN (mchristian.com) is—among many things— an acknowledged master of erotica with more than 25 anthologies and over 300 stories in such collections as *Best American Erotica*, *Best Gay Erotica*, *Best Lesbian Erotica*, *Best Bisexual Erotica*, *Best Fetish Erotica*, and many, many other anthologies, magazines, and websites.

ELIZABETH COLVIN is a journalist and sex educator with a very dirty mind. She bought her first strap-on about ten years ago and became an absolute addict. She loves introducing new men to the joys of strap-on sex. The many notches in her dildos, in fact, form pleasing ridges.

FELIX D'ANGELO's writing has appeared in *MASTER* and *Sweet Life 2*. Also a photographer, his principal interest is a long series of erotic female nudes that just seem to get more explicit with every photo shoot. Taking them is even more fun than writing erotica.

SARA DEMUCI has written for the anthologies *MASTER*, *slave*, and *Down & Dirty*.

ERICA DUMAS has written for *Best Bisexual Women's Erotica*, *Naughty Stories From A to Z*, *G is for Games*, *Open Source Sex*, and the *Sweet Life* series.

ERIC EMERSON had never written erotica before, but he recently developed a desire to do so when putting one of his erotic fantasies down on paper helped it come to fruition. His writing has appeared under other names in various poetry and fiction journals, but this is his first professional erotica sale.

AINSLEIGH FOSTER is a barrista and itinerant business student who discovered once upon a time that his hot girlfriend was doing phone sex secretly to earn extra money, and had decided she liked it. That story was even dirtier than this one.

P. S. HAVEN is from Winston-Salem, North Carolina. His style is heavily influenced by the works of Hugh Hefner, Henry Ford, and David Lee Roth. Haven's stories have been published in the *Best American Erotica* series, *Playing With Fire: Taboo Erotica*, *X: The Erotic Treasury*, *B is for Bondage*, and many others.

JOLIE JOSS is currently a stay-at-home mom who decided to take a foray into erotic literature after hearing some of her husband's more adventurous fantasies. She'd written a number of stories for private enjoyment and has recently enjoyed sharing them with friends. This is her first professional sale.

N. T. MORLEY's more than twenty published and forthcoming novels of erotic dominance and submission are being reprinted in e-book form and can be found at ntmorley.com. Recent and forthcoming novels include *The Biker*, *The Embezzler*, and *The Addendum*; the short story collections include *Captives* and *Master and Slut*.

THOMAS S. ROCHE blogs daily at Techyum.com and monthly at WriteSex.net. His hundreds of published short stories include work in horror, crime fiction, and science fiction as well as erotica. His books include *Noirotica*, *Dark Matter*, and *Parts of Heaven*. His work can be found at www.thomasroche.com.

ISABELLE ROSS has such dirty fantasies that she has to get her boyfriend to make her act them out. Luckily, he's damned good at this. Her work has appeared under various names in several zines, including Mountain Review, Delicious Delusions, and Surprise!

SARAH SANDS is not really a secret sex blogger yet but does share her erotic fantasies with several friends. Since she started that practice, she's been pleased to discover the more you share, the more dirty ideas your friends give you.

DONNA GEORGE STOREY's intimate photography sessions with her husband never stop revealing new pleasures. She is the author of *Amorous Woman*, a steamy tale of an American woman's love affair with Japan, as well as many short stories, which have appeared in *Best Women's Erotica*, *Penthouse*, and *X: The Erotic Treasury*. Read more at DonnaGeorgeStorey.com.

MARIE SUDAC's work has appeared in the anthologies *Best Bisexual Women's Erotica*, *Down & Dirty*, the *Naughty Stories from A to Z* series, and the *Sweet Life* series, as well as at Good-vibes.com and Five Minute Erotica.

Southern California resident **SIMON TORRIO** has written for the anthologies *MASTER* and *Sweet Life 2* and is currently putting the finishing touches on a dark detective novel set in 1930s New Orleans.

SASKIA WALKER (saskiawalker.co.uk) is a British author whose short fiction appears in numerous anthologies. Her erotic novels include *Along for the Ride*, *Rampant*, *Inescapable*, *Monica's Secret*, and *The Harlot*. Saskia lives in the north of England close to the windswept Yorkshire moors, where she happily spends her days spinning yarns.

OSCAR WILLIAMS lives in the Central Valley of California with his wife and their dogs. His work has appeared in the anthology *MASTER*. His erotic novelette about circus clowns became a horror screenplay that is currently being shopped.

About the Editor

VIOLET BLUE (tinynibbles.com, @violetblue) is a Forbes "Web Celeb" and one of Wired's "Faces of Innovation"—in addition to being a blogger, high-profile tech personality, and infamous podcaster. Violet also has many award-winning, best-selling books; an excerpt from her *Smart Girl's Guide to Porn* is featured on Oprah Winfrey's website. She is regarded as the foremost expert in the field of sex and technology, a sex-positive pundit in mainstream media (CNN, "The Oprah Winfrey Show," "The Tyra Banks Show") and is regularly interviewed, quoted, and featured prominently by major media outlets. A published feature writer and columnist since 1998, she also writes for media outlets such as MacLife, *O: The Oprah Magazine*, and the UN-sponsored international health organization RH Reality Check. She was the notorious sex columnist for the *San Francisco Chronicle* with her weekly column "Open Source Sex." She headlines at conferences ranging from ETech, LeWeb, and SXSW: Interactive, to Google Tech Talks at Google, Inc. The *London Times* named Blue "one of the 40 bloggers who really count."